beauty and the beast

VIVIENNE SAVAGE

ALSO BY VIVIENNE SAVAGE

DAWN OF THE DRAGONS

Loved by the Dragon

Smitten

Crush

THE WILD OPERATIVES

The Right to Bear Arms

Let Us Prey

The Purr-fect Soldier

Old Dog, New Tricks

THE WOLVES OF SAN ANTONIO

Training the Alpha

IMPRACTICAL MAGIC

Impractical Magic: A Halloween Prequel

Better Than Hex (Coming Soon)

MYTHOLOGICAL LOVERS

Making Waves

Dedicated to the readers who made this possible. Thank you for buying, sharing, and reviewing. Thank you for your word of mouth praise to your friends and family. And most of all, thank you to my wonderful PA, Laura Trujillo for putting up with my crap at two in the morning.

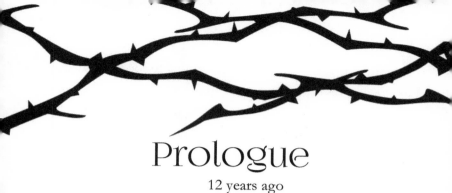

Prologue

12 years ago

GOLDEN LIGHT SHONE over the mountaintop garden, but even its gilded beauty failed to soothe Alistair's rage. Smoke stained the sky in the far distance, barely a smudge to his eye. Another village in the neighboring kingdom of Dalborough had burned to the ground.

"You've killed innocents, Alistair. What did those people do to deserve such a cruel fate?"

Sparkling motes on the breeze coalesced together, creating a human-sized feminine form wrapped in silver filaments. The fairy Eos fluttered to the ground on iridescent wings, standing eye level with the prince to meet him as his equal.

"Everything," Alistair hissed. "Were my people not innocent? Were the villagers slaughtered by the king's army not deserving of a chance at life? Their black wizard cursed our land. Those who survived cannot sprout even a single bean in this soil and slowly starve, yet you wish me to forgive Dalborough for these wrongs?"

"You picked a fight with commoners. You condemned people to death for the mere crime of being human, knowing battle would weigh favorably to your advantage. Have you forgotten your own people? That they look to you for guidance and protection while you abandon them and harass the western kingdom in your futile, one-sided war?" she asked in a voice simmering with fury. "The battle has ended, Alistair. Your mother would bow her head in shame. You disgrace her memory, and I cannot allow this farce to continue."

"Eos—"

"My mind is made up. I have watched you shirk your father's duties while in pursuit of vengeance. The murderer of your parents is no longer a threat, and many years will pass before their army recovers. You are now the monster."

"I sought justice!" he argued. "Where were you when the humans slew my family? Killed our people and destroyed our villages? Where were you then, fairy?"

A frigid lance of power paralyzed Alistair, rooting him to the spot. Every inch of him ached, down to the core of his bones where it radiated out to his strong appendages. In the blink of an eye, the dragon shifter had assumed his larger form. Against his will. He'd never experienced a forced transformation in all of his life, but the fairy had thrust him into his dragon body with the ease of plucking a flower from the garden.

"What have you done to me?"

"If thou wish to behave like a beast, then a beast thou shall be," she whispered, fading away on the wind. "Until true love is found to see the human in thee."

Alistair attempted to leap into his human shape, but when nothing happened, he rocked back onto his haunches to stare at her disappearing form. "Eos, don't do this. Don't trap me this way."

"What need do you have of a human body if your hatred of their kind has grown so greatly, Alistair?" The silken voice carried on the breeze then her voice rose in volume, and the ground quaked from the fairy's power. "Thirteen years this curse shall endure, these grounds revived and castle secure."

"Eos! Wait!" he cried. "You cannot do this to me! I'm your godson!"

The awe-inspiring power of the fairies was known across the many kingdoms, and the weight of the curse hanging over his head struck him with terror. Those who failed to meet their requirements of a fairy's curse were men who died.

Thirteen years.

The winds swirled around him, and his dragon's skin tingled anew with magic. He sagged on the spot as the spell wound itself in place, sizzling into his soul. He had been sentenced to a slow, thirteen-year death sentence, and he was powerless to stop her.

"Weep not, Prince Alistair. All is not lost, for there is no magic without a cost. A princess will come of her own free will. Say nothing of the truth, and her heart thou shall steal. Beautiful inside and out, her hair will smolder like the sun, and in time she will realize thine heart is the one."

He tried to protest again, twisting around to search the winds for her, but she was gone with a final whispered echo.

One chance. The mystery princess would be his only

VIVIENNE SAVAGE

chance.

Now if only he knew her name and where to find her.

Chapter 1

THE DWINDLING SUN fell upon Anastasia's hair, transforming her auburn mane into strands of fire. An afternoon ride with her cousin had been the remedy to a dull day in the lonely castle, despite the royal escort lurking to their rear out of earshot.

"I'll pass," Anastasia said.

"Prince Joren is an absolute dream. Are you not interested in meeting him?" Victoria asked, flabbergasted.

"Prince Joren is an absolute royal ass," Anastasia retorted ruefully. "I've already met him at the Midsummer Gala, where he couldn't keep his bloody eyes away from my cleavage long enough to enjoy his meal."

"You're exaggerating."

"I've seen nursing tots less interested in breasts," Ana mused. "Besides, I don't mind that he looked, but I do mind that he wasn't able to look away."

"Aside from his poor table manners and interest in your breasts, there had to be something positive about the meeting."

"He's an accomplished war mage and studied at the Collegium in the north."

Victoria sighed. "Of all the qualities to admire in a man,

you find the least interesting of them all. Who cares where he's gone to study?"

Anastasia winked. "What isn't interesting about an educated man able to set fire to his enemies?"

Of course, she had no interest in Joren beyond appreciating the view, not that she'd ever admit the handsome young prince had come close to captivating her. Contrary to what she told her friend, she'd been quite smitten until he told her women in his father's kingdom weren't permitted to learn magic beyond hearth and home.

Anastasia's father, King Morgan, ran their kingdom differently. As a child, she'd lived for the days when he held court, claiming she wanted to learn to be a fair and just ruler like him one day. Then her mother would discourage her, promising she'd excel as a pretty queen to stand at her husband's side instead.

At least, Queen Lorelei had once counseled her daughter to that effect, years ago when she could still speak without uttering gibberish. Before her illness, the queen had been an exceptional seer without equal, guiding generals, leaders of the clergy, and even her husband. If not for the witnesses present for Anastasia's birth, no one would believe Ana and her mother were related at all. Lorelei was dark-haired and a fragile contrast to the regal king with his fair skin, brawny build, and steel gray goatee.

Anastasia didn't resemble either parent, being petite and chubby until squeezed into a corset. Throw in the red hair, and anyone could confuse her for a changeling swapped at birth by the fairies.

But her coloring was the least of the differences between Anastasia and her parents. She glowered down at her thighs. They were full and thick, snugly held by the riding pants she fancied while on horseback. She preferred to ride like a man, straddling the horse.

To her right, Victoria rode sidesaddle, dressed in a multi-layered but breezy dress and summer hat. The wide brim shaded her porcelain complexion, and she made the perfect example of a noble lady.

"Enough about me. Tell me about your evening with Sir Bryant. How was it?"

Victoria shrugged and focused on the path ahead. Her unenthused eyes and flat mouth told Anastasia everything she needed to know.

"Oh, Vicky, I'm sorry, love."

"It's nothing. There'll be other suitors."

Anastasia nodded and steered her horse closer until the mares nearly touched ribs and she could take one of Victoria's gloved hands. "We'll be old maids together then, won't we?"

Victoria chuckled and squeezed her fingers. "Yes, of course. I heard it's all the rage these days to remain forever young and beautiful, untethered by marriage and unaged by children."

"You'll certainly have fewer wrinkles. But do you know what else'll give you fewer wrinkles?"

VIVIENNE SAVAGE

"What?" Victoria asked, giggling.

"An eve away from the dilemma of being Lady Victoria. Do you trust me?"

"Of course I do."

The giggles ended as they separated and Anastasia urged her horse into a burst of speed. Victoria followed, and together they raced down the hill, leaving a startled royal guard in their dust. Her soot-gray mare and Victoria's black beauty were too fast for the nervous man to keep pace behind them. With her hair flying in the wind and the relaxing motion of a horse beneath her, Anastasia sailed to the palace gates.

"Can we lose him?" Victoria asked.

"I'm certain of it. Quick, follow me!" Ana called.

A handsome city watchman stood beside the open gates, but his expression of warmth melted into a confused stare. His partner, a broad-shouldered, hulking giant of a man in matching, dark boiled leather armor, pointed to the royal escort pursuing them.

"Ana, they're not moving!"

"They'll move!" Ana shouted back.

They did. After lingering until the very last minute, as if hoping to intimidate the girls into halting their escape, both men dove out of the way. Ana and Victoria hurried into the city and turned a sharp left into the markets. Their lithe horses navigated the narrow rows between shop stalls with ease.

The markets of Creag Morden were a maze for the unprepared, but they were also the best place to become lost.

They twisted their mares into the next street and down a narrow path behind the shops.

"How are we going to lose them?" Victoria asked above the din of startled voices.

"With magic! We have a bit of a lead on them. Hurry and dismount. They'll be here soon!"

Anastasia sent the two horses ahead without them. They watched the elegant beasts gallop away, riderless, but instructed to return home. They'd reach the castle gates within minutes to be received by puzzled guards.

"Hold my hands," Anastasia instructed. "I'll hide us."

"Can you do it?" Victoria asked, a combination of enthusiasm and fear seeping into her voice. "I can't believe we're doing this." The girl glanced up and down the alley as they joined hands. "It's so exciting. I've never done anything like this before."

"Neither have I."

The young women stood still together for a time as Anastasia pushed outward with her magic. Moments later, the guardsmen sped by, their feet pounding the hard-packed street. They disappeared around the corner in pursuit of the horses.

"It worked," Anastasia said, surprised.

"Did you honestly doubt yourself?"

"A little," she admitted.

"Ana, darling, you made us invisible."

Anastasia shook her head. "I cast a spell to make us

inconspicuous, not invisible. There's no telling what they saw. The mind makes up what it wants. They probably saw two washerwomen or a pair of beggars."

"And *that's* easier than making us invisible?"

Ana gave her friend an impish grin. "Definitely. Now let's go before they circle around again to look for us. You once told me you'd love to visit the seediest bar in the city, and with a clever disguise, we can enjoy a few hours of sweet anonymity." Wearing a big grin on her face, Ana held up a satchel of clothing.

In a matter of minutes, they were able to bribe a pair of young peasant girls into swapping dresses, then they stormed the poor quarter of the city while wearing enough makeup on their faces to rival the streetwalkers. The girls drank cheap wine, imbibed on honey mead, and had the time of their lives as a pair of normal city girls.

"Should we feel bad about the men out looking for us?"

"No," Ana answered. "Father pays them well. They're earning their keep, and he's always said the whole lot of them are only getting fat without any true work to do."

"Point well made. This must be the most excitement they've had all year."

They returned to the castle long after dark while the city watch combed the streets. By then, the girls had wiped the makeup from their faces and let down their hair again from their hastily plaited peasant braids.

So much for the dangers of the peasantry, Ana thought.

According to her mother, she ought to have been abused and in a ditch hours ago. Returning unharmed and wholly intact to the castle gave her a smug sense of satisfaction that her parents were wrong.

The guard on duty at the gate did a double take when the two young women approached arm in arm and giggling like loons. "Princess Anastasia? Lady Victoria?" He promptly rang the bell, the gates parted, and then the castle doors opened beyond the courtyard to reveal several quickly moving figures. Her father was at the lead, red-faced and furious.

"We've returned," Anastasia said cheerfully.

"Where have you been? Half of the royal guard has gone looking for you."

"I went to enjoy a fun evening without a grim-faced guardian standing over my shoulder. Is that too much to ask for, Father? I promise, we were both perfectly safe the entire while. See? We came to no harm."

"You both smell like a distillery."

The girls tittered, leaning on each other for support.

"A few drinks is all, no worse than the usual feasts we've hosted at the castle." *Please don't be angry, don't be angry*, she thought.

"Do you not realize the depth of the trouble this little excursion has caused? That the guard and I feared for your safety? Williford was beside himself with worry and blamed himself most of all for your loss. He has traveled the streets for hours. *Hours*, Anastasia, calling your name, taking aside any citizen who may have seen your face."

Anastasia sighed. Her bubble of pride popped, and the elation whistled away on the breeze. Of all the things she'd wanted from her tour, terrifying her father hadn't been among them. She'd only wanted to know what it was like to travel freely, like one of her brothers, without a man lurking behind her.

"I'm sorry for worrying you, Father. I never meant to make you or Sir Williford afraid for us. I wasn't thinking." But I don't apologize for enjoying a day alone.

"And then you involve poor Victoria in your strange machinations. Her mother and father haven't had a moment's rest since this debacle began."

"I'm sorry, Papa, I didn't mean to frighten anyone. I only wanted a moment of peace with Victoria."

As the guilt needled Ana, she felt Victoria squeeze her hand. No matter the carefree fun they'd had, she still felt like an ass for dragging her friend along into trouble.

King Morgan's features softened. "I've chastised you both enough. Come inside now, my daughter."

They trailed behind the king with their hands still joined, forced to take quicker strides to keep up with his brisk pace.

"No matter what's said, I came with you of my own free will," Victoria whispered to her. "And I don't regret that. We had an amazing time today, Anastasia. Never forget."

"I won't," she whispered back to her friend. "Today, we were normal girls."

"Today, we had the time of our lives," Victoria agreed with a smile.

King Morgan forgave Anastasia's transgression, but he didn't forget. Despite her promises to never repeat her escape, he increased the number of guardsmen surrounding her. She spent days playing the part of the doting daughter, behaving as a proper princess should, and apologizing for her behavior.

But no amount of genuine repentance could dampen her desire to see beyond the castle gates again, to explore a world on her own. Attempts to talk to him on the matter met outright refusal.

"You don't understand how much the thought of losing you terrifies me, Anastasia. You are my one and only daughter. The world out there isn't meant for you. You must stay here where you're safe, protected, and kept from harm," the king explained.

Of all the rooms in the palace, Ana loved the library the most. Her parents had accumulated a varied collection over the years, and her earliest memories involved playing on the rug in front of the hearth while her mother read fables and fairy tales to her.

She and her father each occupied their usual seats, his chair a massive construction of wood and leather, hers a pink and cream velvet chaise. Her mother's chair remained empty, and had for some time. Lorelei hadn't stepped foot in the

VIVIENNE SAVAGE

library for a year at least. She hadn't read a book in over three.

"Whatever will you do once I've left to attend the Collegium, Father? Who will worry you then?"

"Then I will direct my concerns to the rest of your unmarried siblings."

Ana scoffed and refrained from voicing a retort. The rest of her brothers were all younger, with distinguished matches negotiated between their allies in neighboring kingdoms.

Often, when she was alone with her thoughts, she blamed her magic for his overprotectiveness. Did he worry she would end up like her mother, broken and raving?

Ana's desire to learn conquered any fear of the unknown future. She craved knowledge, and most of all, she loved the sparks of magic around her fingertips, an ever-present reminder of the gift she'd inherited from her fairy grandmother.

A royal guardsman cleared his throat from the entrance of the audience chamber. "Your Grace, there is a man here to see you. One of the mercenaries you employed."

"Good, send him in. Anastasia, my dear, please—"

"Can I stay, Father? Please. If they've come with good tidings, I want to hear as well."

"You only wish to see the flower," the king retorted.

Shortly after the onset of her mother's dementia, the king had developed an unnatural, unhealthy obsession with the sky forests of the Benthwaite Mountains to the east, claiming the verdant peaks of the adjacent land hid an immeasurable wealth in medicinal cures. He never missed an opportunity to share the stories his father once told him about the travelers who journeyed to the ancient caves for raw gemstones. According to his tales, a rare rose grew only in the shadow of the mountain's highest steppe, in the garden of an abandoned castle.

He sent explorers at first, and when none returned, he sent his best combat scouts. His devoted men posted notices around the kingdom's tap houses until a group of experienced men and women boisterously promised they'd claim the mountains in his name.

A pale man entered the library, a shadow of the arrogant warrior who promised to stake the king's banner on the mountain peak. He shook and trembled, smelling like hell itself. Ana fought the urge to wrinkle her nose.

"Well?" her father demanded without preamble. "Where is the flower?"

"Sire, it cannot be done. A dragon inhabits the mountain."

A dragon! The thought made her head spin and produced romantic images of dragons soaring through the skies. The majestic beasts hadn't been seen in Creag Morden for decades despite warring with their southern neighbors in Dalborough.

"Did I not pay you to slay the beast if such a creature was encountered?"

"You did, Your Highness, but he cannot be slain by any conventional means. He is powerful beyond anything we have ever seen. We lost two of our band before our archer released his first arrow!"

VIVIENNE SAVAGE

"Such casualties are expected."

Her father's cool, callous words drew her startled gaze. The mercenary bowed his head, his hand clenching at his sides.

"Indeed, they are, but we had no choice but to retreat lest we all lose our lives."

King Morgan exploded from his seat and slammed both hands against the table. Tea sloshed over the rim of her cup, and she flinched as his voice boomed across the library. "You retreated?"

Anastasia watched the trembling man. Ash darkened his perspiring face, and his body odor filled the room with the smell of soot and blood.

"Of course we did, Your Highness. We value our skins more than gold."

"And where's the rest of your party?"

"Traveling south. And I shall now join them. The beast gave us but one day's head start to leave these lands and to give you this message."

King Morgan's brows raised. "He sent you with a message?"

"Aye, he did." The mercenary hesitated. "He says he's been kind, sire, but press your luck again, and he'll rain fire upon your kingdom then gnaw your bones."

Upon delivering his message, the man fled the room. From a window overlooking the courtyard, Anastasia saw him mount his sweaty horse and gallop away without looking back.

"I hired cowards," her father seethed. "Useless, yellow-bellied cowards."

"Papa, everyone across the kingdom knows how much you love Mother and that you've done all of this for her, but have you considered that maybe the healers are right? Maybe it's irreversible, and the queen we've both known is gone forever."

"I refuse to believe as much."

"Father, how many more will you send to their doom? What if this flower can do nothing for her and you've undertaken an impossible mission?"

King Morgan shook his head. "That is where you are wrong, my darling. Nothing is impossible, and with faith, we can accomplish anything."

The king excused himself from their tea time and met with his chief steward to increase the bounty on the dragon.

The first dragon slayer visited the palace on a bright summer morning, a fortnight after the famous explorers fled Creag Morden. His steps thundered over the marble, his plate armor an enormous addition to a body already swollen with muscle.

Anastasia stared at him during the introduction. A trio of identical scars slashed across his scalp and over the man's brow, the third bisecting it neatly. Puckered, shiny pink flesh arose from the collar of his plate armor.

She shuddered.

"It is an honor to stand before you, King Morgan. I am Henry Galway of Kirkwall." The knight bowed to her father

VIVIENNE SAVAGE

then pivoted to give her the same prompt consideration. "Princess."

"Ah, yes. Word has reached me of your skill and vast knowledge for dispatching these creatures."

"I have killed many," the knight agreed. "What may I claim as a prize when I slay this one?"

"Ten thousand crowns," her father named without blinking.

"Not only will I skin it prior to immolation, but I'll bring its claws for your trophy room, Your Highness."

The knight bowed to them both then strode from the throne room, his heavy armor clanking noisily.

Anastasia watched him leave with a feeling of dread. Something deep in her gut told her killing their dragon would be easier said than done. And if this knight failed, they would all pay for it in blood.

Victoria rapidly fanned the air in front of her face, as if it could further cool the dais from where she and Anastasia spectated the annual games over tea. Under normal circumstances, the King himself would preside over the races, but he'd withdrawn from society and sent his daughter in his stead.

Too busy plotting and scheming over how to take on Benthwaite, she thought. It wasn't that she didn't wish her father well, but that she believed the healers who swore no amount of herbal remedies would cure her mother's ailment.

Despite their past tension, there wasn't anything Anastasia wouldn't give to have her mother restored if it was in her power. But it wasn't. And as far as she was concerned, her father was going to get a lot of good people killed.

Benthwaite was once known for an abundance of dragons, and where there was one, there had to be more. She imagined a horde of hatchlings in a dank, overgrown cave, warmed beneath their mother's scaly body until the next group of hapless humans came stumbling in for treasure.

"Ana, my dear? Are you quite all right, love?" Lady Victoria asked.

Anastasia snapped out of her thoughts and turned her attention to her company. "My apologies. My mind is filled with heavy thoughts."

"Say nothing more of it. Has your father received news from his dragonslayer?"

The princess shook her head. "Nothing since he was sighted crossing the border."

"Pity. Maybe if the dragons of Benthwaite were exterminated, prosperity could be brought to this desolate little kingdom again." She sighed and fanned her face.

"I don't know," Ana said. "The dragons don't trouble anyone until they're bothered, or so the old tales say. When was the last time anyone's actually witnessed an attack from them?"

"Years ago, and nowhere near Creag Morden," Victoria

VIVIENNE SAVAGE

admitted. "But for all we know, they're waiting and biding their time. They're cunning beasts, are they not? Hoarding such precious treasures all to themselves when they have no better use for them."

Were humans any better? Anastasia had her doubts about it, but she erred on the side of caution and pointed, changing the subject by saying, "Oh, look! What a darling pony."

Two knights charged one another on horseback, each holding a shield and a lance leveled toward his opponent. Thundering hooves sent up a fine cloud of dust around strong equine legs.

"Dear, the worth of that war charger exceeds the cost of the dress on your body. Both of our bodies. Hardly a po—"

The bell tolled from the eastern watchtowers at the outskirts of the city.

"That's the emergency bell, isn't it?" Victoria asked.

"It is, though I wonder why."

A scream pierced the raucous din of commoners in the cramped stands, and all eyes turned toward the shrieking woman pointing east. The celebratory music trumpeting through the air came to an abrupt halt.

Anastasia leaned from her seat and twisted for a better look. With the sun in her eyes, she could hardly see. "Is that—" Her eyes grew wide. In the distance, a winged behemoth grew increasingly large.

"It couldn't be," Victoria whispered.

The announcer dashed to his pedestal. "Ladies and

gentlemen, you must leave here and find safety at once. There isn't a moment to lose!"

A sweaty, red-faced guard rushed up the steps to the covered dais. "Your Highness! A dragon approaches!"

Victoria clutched a hand to her breast. "What do we do? Where do we go?"

"The castle, my lady. Please, a carriage awaits the both of you."

With no alternative but to obey, the two women hurried to the carriage and clung to one another as the doors slammed shut. Seconds later, the vehicle lurched forward.

"Can't these beasts gallop any faster?" the guard hissed.

Although she couldn't see through the wooden walls behind her, Ana had the distinct feeling the dragon was closing in on them, a theory confirmed once the carriage sped onto the courtyard and the doors opened.

Men stood at the ballistas, preparing them for war. Victoria sobbed beside her as she rushed for the opening castle doors, and in the distance, the dragon's immense shape grew larger and larger with each heartbeat slamming in Ana's chest. The blood rushed in her ears, the sound of her own pulse deafening over the screams of the men moving into their positions. They were ready to die to defend the castle.

And it was unnecessary. All of their preparation was in vain.

The dragon soared by on magnificent ruby wings but waged no assault on the palace. As he passed the courtyard, the monster dropped a charred lump of metal. Sir Henry, welded within his armor and long dead, resembled a piece of coal melded with blackened steel. After a defiant roar, the beast flew away and was soon out of sight.

King Morgan strode past both girls without a word. Anastasia watched him approach the unmoving corpse. He stared at it, trembling with rage.

The message was quite clear.

"Send word to the other kingdoms. This beast will die. No request is too great, no price too high. I will grant anything to the man who puts an end to this dragon."

Chapter 2

King Morgan's audience chamber became quiet over the weeks following Henry's demise. While he didn't grieve for the brave knight, he certainly appeared to mourn the loss of a chance to raid Benthwaite. Like a greedy buzzard, he waited to descend upon the carcass of the mountain once its protector had been slain.

One by one, men died in the pursuit of treasure beyond their wildest dreams and a promise of more gold crowns than they could reasonably spend in their lifetime.

The next adventurer, a quiet, thoughtful man from Liang, listened as the king described his troubles and said he would only accept payment upon completion of the job.

"This dragon, it must be a young dragon," the stranger said, stroking his black mustache with his thumb.

"I care not of its age. I care that it is killed soon," her father said.

"I will need time to prepare for this, but I can dispatch your creature. I will require much time."

Weeks passed, but he never returned.

The fifth respondent arrived on an overcast Sunday afternoon. Ana knew he had to be a *prestigious* member of some royal family when the servants began to fret and hastily flutter about the palace like chickens with lost heads, clucking over his handsome qualities, the wealth of his kingdom, and his bachelor status.

"Your father requests your company, milady."

"Oh? What for?"

"He's received a visit from Prince Edward of Dalborough, and they both would like to speak with you presently! Isn't this wonderful, your highness? Now is your chance," the maid said in a dreamy whisper. She held her hand over her heart and sighed. "He's a catch of enormous quality. Their royal family has grown prosperous over the years, *and* he is quite attractive."

"Is he?" Ana asked, skeptical.

The maid sighed. "His eyes, they're stunning, like chips of cobalt or sapphire."

Ana shook her head. She'd settle for a prince who was kind to his subjects. Prince Edward and his family had a terrible reputation for lining their pockets with gold while their commoners starved.

"Help me dress please?" she said lightly, forcing a smile to her face. Once skirted and laced into her bodice, she ran a brush through her hair and stepped into a pair of soft, velvet-lined slippers. The gold color suited her and matched her favorite dress for receiving esteemed visitors.

"They await you on the veranda."

Anastasia's brows squeezed together. That was unusual.

"Thank you, Clara."

Under normal circumstances, her father reserved the veranda for close friends and relatives.

Frowning every step of the way, she took the route to the castle's upper-level veranda. She found her father and the prince seated side by side like old pals around a small table laden with regional delicacies and wine.

"Allow me to introduce you to my only daughter, Anastasia Rose. Ana, darling, meet Prince Edward of Dalborough."

"The pleasure is mine," Edward greeted her in genial tones, his voice a smooth baritone. He rose from the seat and bowed before taking her offered hand.

Her heart lurched in her chest when his lips grazed her knuckles. The servants weren't wrong. Handsome didn't begin to describe him.

The prince guided her to his right and took the chair between Ana and her father. She frowned.

"And also mine, Prince Edward. To what pleasure do we owe such a fine visit?"

"Word came to my mother and father concerning the recent troubles in Creag Morden. My parents believe we could come to an agreement regarding aid. A union."

"Ahh, Edward, much time has passed since we've last held words together. Tell me about your mother and father; are they well?" her father asked.

"Quite well, Your Highness. They send their apologies, but prior obligations have kept them from accompanying me."

VIVIENNE SAVAGE

"Of course. There will be other opportunities in the future," King Morgan said.

With a feeling of unease pervading Ana's mood, she quieted to sip tea.

"If I recall, your father slew the wyrm of Cairn Ocland during the Great War of the Beasts."

And it begins, Ana thought, disgusted. She prepared a small plate of food for herself and nibbled on a pastry as an excuse to remain silent.

"He did, although it was the battle to end his career," Edward replied. "Before him, my great-grandfather killed the wyrm of Liang."

"Excellent. Have you inherited their talent for slaying dragons?"

"The rarity of dragons has presented a bit of a challenge, so I remain untested. When news of your difficulties reached our kingdom, we decided to extend the kind offer to exterminate your beast, King Morgan."

"I have hired many men to try and take down this creature. Even a warrior from Liang. I received word that he will be ready to attack within the month."

Edward chuckled. "He can certainly try, but would you not rather rely on your neighbors?"

The king retained his smile, wearing the polite expression as he would don a mask for a masquerade ball. Ana knew her father well enough to recognize when he loathed someone on sight. "Will there be a cost, or shall I assume this is an act of benevolence?"

"Perhaps the terms of this arrangement may prove beneficial to both of our families. It may be the greatest cost you will ever pay, and also the least."

The king's eyes lit with interest. "Speak, son. What price do you ask?"

"Your daughter's hand in marriage." Prince Edward's cunning smile reminded Anastasia of a fox who had wormed his way into a hen house.

With his dark, curly hair and bright blue eyes, most women would be delighted to accept his offer. Edward's shoulders weren't as broad as the deceased Sir Henry's immense frame, but she imagined an attractive athleticism beneath his blue, gold-stitched tunic. And muscles. Muscles she could touch and trace to her heart's content. She'd only glimpsed illustrations in a library book, her knowledge of the male form minimal at best.

"I understand the princess is magically gifted," Prince Edward began, never taking his eyes off her. "Is she as talented as her mother?"

"More talented," King Morgan said.

"I don't—"

"Anastasia has developed an incredible sense of modesty," her father interrupted, cutting her off.

"Magic is highly prized in Dalborough. She would have access to the finest magical institutions and grandest libraries beyond her imagination."

"Please do not speak about me as if I'm not present," Ana cut in. "I've already written my acceptance letter to the Collegium, and Father's—"

The king interrupted her. "Yes, excellent point, Edward. You have my word that if you succeed in killing this beast, you'll have my daughter's hand in marriage."

Anastasia whipped her head around to stare at her father. Her mouth opened and shut wordlessly. Betrayal stung, as intense as a lance driven through her heart.

"Father, you promised!"

Both men carried on as if she hadn't spoken at all.

"Ah, but King Morgan, certainly we can agree upon a marriage to take place before I march with the army to the mountains. My men will fight with greater zeal knowing they fight for their new princess and with strong allies behind them."

King Morgan rubbed his chin to contemplate the offer. "A wise plan, young man. Very wise indeed. And the man I've already hired?"

"We will gladly help pay the price for his assistance in the matter if he succeeds before our army arrives."

"Agreed."

How could he do it? It was the worst sort of betrayal, and the last thing she expected.

"Has no one cared to ask what I want?" Ana twisted in her seat to stare at her suitor. "I am sorry to disappoint you, Prince Edward, but I have little desire to become wed. And I hardly know you. We have only just met!"

"We once played together as children. Do you not remember?"

Anastasia studied his face, her memories tugged by a faint recollection of a curly-haired boy who tossed mud at her dress and possibly tried to make her eat a bug. Neither memory endeared him to her. "Nothing pleasant," she retorted before turning to face King Morgan. "Father, you can't do this. How could you even entertain the thought of arranging a marriage to their family when you've promised I would be allowed to attend the Collegium?"

He didn't look at her when he replied, avoiding eye contact. That cut the deepest. "I know."

"They've accepted me. Please, you mustn't do this," she pleaded.

In a weary voice, the king replied, "My daughter, the time has come to grow up and face reality. To take on some responsibilities."

With the prince sitting between them, she couldn't take her father's hands and make him look at her. Couldn't appeal to his heart. Each time she leaned forward and tried, she saw only Edward's smug face.

"Why? Why do this to me?"

"Because you're my little princess, Ana, and I want nothing but the best for you. You deserve more than a half-life in your mother's shadow. The time has come for you to leave Creag Morden behind to find a life of your own in a new

VIVIENNE SAVAGE

home."

"This *is* my home! My entire life is here, Father. Here with you and my family."

"And soon, you will have another," Edward said without losing his condescending smile. As a testament to her inner strength, Ana found the mental control over her emotions to practice self-restraint. Slapping the smirk from his face would only cause trouble.

Her father nodded in agreement. "A protected life with no need of magic. So long as I draw breath, you will never share your mother's fate."

"You are sorely mistaken if you believe I'll meet you at the altar," Ana said succinctly to the prince. She rose from the seat and strode from the veranda to keep her dignity intact.

The betrothal was a beautiful success despite all efforts made by Anastasia to ruin her own impending nuptials. When flat out refusal failed to sway her father, he took away her spellbooks and barred her from the castle library. It didn't break her. Instead, she grew more determined until he threatened to send her to a convent.

She called his bluff until a nun arrived to speak about her devotion to the Creator.

Invitations flew to every corner of the three civilized kingdoms, and Creag Morden's best dressmaker created a golden vision for her to wear on her special day. Defeated,

Anastasia went along with their plans to become the trophy wife of Prince Edward, future Queen of Dalborough.

Three days of silence in the coach frayed her nerves. Victoria hadn't been allowed to accompany her, and Ana refused to speak with her father. Struck by an unusual fit of silence, her mother spent the duration of their travel gazing out the window.

At night when they stopped at a bed and breakfast, royal guards stood by Anastasia's door.

Did he expect her to flee on Sterling in the middle of the night?

The very moment she reached Darkmoor Castle and saw the smug bastard awaiting her on the castle steps, she regretted the decision to decline the convent.

She regretted it even more when her future in-laws spoke over her at their first family dinner.

King Frederick terrified her, and his golden-haired wife gazed down her long and narrow, haughty nose. Each time she questioned them about enrolling in one of their fine magical institutions, the king changed the subject or his queen asked about her beauty regime. What she thought of her new bedroom. If she'd considered dyeing her hair before the ceremony; red was such an awful color.

The king glowered from his seat at the head of the table, his face a mask of pink-scarred agony. During the Great War of the Beasts, he had slain the Witch Queen's dragon mount, but at a great price. His looks and his left arm had been lost.

VIVIENNE SAVAGE

Most of his features ran together, like a wax doll melted under the sunlight.

She did her best not to stare, but her other options were limited and no better. Across the table, her future spouse gazed at her with bedroom eyes.

Feigning illness, Anastasia begged their excuse from the table and retired to her bedchamber where she didn't emerge until the following day for her dress fitting.

Then the hunger strike resumed, and she retired early to bed with hours left until her wedding. At noon, she'd become another possession of Darkmoor Castle. The quality of her mind would be forgotten, and her worth would be measured by how many children she could bear her husband.

A sharp rap at the door interrupted Ana as she removed the silver, emerald-dotted pins from her hair. At home, Lorissa or Vera would have taken down her hair, and she missed them dearly.

"Princess Anastasia, may I enter?" Edward called.

At this hour? Startled, she drew her dressing gown around her and cracked open the door. "Is it not inappropriate to be without a chaperone, my lord?"

"We are to be married tomorrow. Such things are no longer a concern," he assured her before a wide smile spread across his face.

Anastasia leaned into the hall and glanced up both ends of the empty corridor. There wasn't a person in sight.

"I asked the guards to step aside and grant us some time

to talk."

"So I see."

"Is the room to your liking?" Edward asked as he made his way inside.

"It's very—" She searched for a polite word. "—plain for a bride's new bedchamber."

Her new home differed in multiple ways from the palace of her childhood, dark and ostentatious with few windows, a prison of cold, black stone. Even the stoic-faced castle guards reminded her of the wardens in Creag Morden's jail.

An impersonal bedroom surrounded her, lacking warmth in its bleak design. From the gray, silk sheets to the dreary curtains bordering the tiny windows, the cheerless atmosphere made her long for the comfort of home.

"Arrangements could be made if you desire."

Anastasia exhaled in relief. "Thank you."

"It is no trouble." His arm curled around her waist; then he drew her close, pressing her against the lean, hard frame of his body. She froze and wiggled free to back away.

"My, my, you are a shy little thing. Don't be afraid, little Ana, we're to be married tomorrow."

"Exactly. Tomorrow," she stressed.

"No one would look down on us getting to know one another a little early." He tugged on her again, drawing her back toward him. "No one will know, after all. The guards have been instructed to remain away for hours, my dear. Hours."

Gut instinct told her to demand him to leave or put his

claims to the test by screaming.

"I'm not ready."

"Oh? And in one day you shall be?"

"I may not be ready tomorrow night either," she admitted. "As I said before, we may have played as children, but I no longer know you. I'd like the time to adjust to these changes."

Edward was dangerously cute, but the attraction ended at his physical attributes. As far as she could see, he was just another hot prince with breathtaking eyes and a smarmy grin.

"Do you truly believe we could end the night chaste after our wedding?" His brittle chuckle lacked humor, sounding darker and more foreboding by the passing second. "Kiss me."

"I will kiss you tomorrow," she reminded him.

"What harm is there in one little kiss from a bride-to-be to her future husband?" he challenged.

Ana bit her lower lip thoughtfully and hung back a step.

"One kiss, and then I would like to retire for an eve of rest before our wedding day, please."

Edward grinned back at her. "Agreed."

She reluctantly stepped forward and risked a look into his eyes. They were gorgeous, as her friends and maids often told her, the shade reminding her of a still lake beneath a cloudless sky. His jaw and chin were smooth shaven, but a few waves of his dark hair rested over his forehead. The boyish look conflicted with the muscles beneath his tunic.

Kissing her roughly, the prince swept his tongue between her lips, and the sharp, sweet taste of white wine filled her mouth. His strong arms crushed her close, introducing her to chiseled, masculine angles defined by his talent with a sword. There was no doubt about it; he was a strong man, and most women would consider themselves lucky to have him for their betrothed.

"Mm…." Edward moaned when she ended the kiss and turned her face into his cheek. "Was that so horrible?"

To the contrary, she'd enjoyed it more than expected. It gave her hope of one day acquiring genuine feelings. Years later, she wanted to be laughing while telling her children how close she'd come to missing out on the love of her life.

"No," she admitted. "Goodnight, Edward. Shall we meet in the morning for breakfast before the ceremony?"

"Breakfast?" he echoed, staring at her dumbfounded. He'd expected more.

After spending a few heartbeats on the receiving end of a dirty stare, Anastasia dipped her head to look away. "Tomorrow is a new day. We'll get to know one another, and once this is no longer terrifying, maybe…." She bit her lower lip and ignored the heavy feeling at the bottom of her belly. "I'm very sorry that this doesn't feel right this evening, Edward."

Finished with giving apologies, she stepped away, only for Edward to yank her back by the wrist. The recoil threw her off balance and sent her crashing into his chest.

"You must be daft if you believe I'll accept a no after waiting weeks to be wed to you."

"Let go of me."

  VIVIENNE SAVAGE

"No." If anything, he squeezed a little tighter until the tips of her fingers tingled.

"I haven't asked for much. A few days to know you—"

"Grow up," he snarled at her. "You are so very far from home now. And you're mine."

"I may be far from home, but I am still the daughter of a king," Anastasia stated plainly, her observation seeming to incense Edward more than her refusal. "You have absolutely lost your mind if you believe me to be some possession you've attained through marriage. My father would never stand for this sort of behavior."

"Your father is no longer in the castle!" he crowed victoriously. "He left. He and your dimwitted mother."

Anastasia twisted out of his sweaty grip and rushed for the door, but Edward caught her before she made an escape into the hall.

"Someone help! Please, hel—" She bounced off the door as he captured her by a handful of hair and crashed her head against it. An explosion of pain bloomed behind her brow, and she staggered backward toward the center of the room.

Then she was face down on the bed with his weight on the back of her knees and the fluffy blankets muffling her cries. He had a hand around her throat, squeezing the air from her lungs until she could barely draw the breath to scream.

The more she struggled, the more it hurt.

"I knew you'd see things my way," Edward muttered once Anastasia surrendered to his greater power, making little noise beyond thirsty gasps for air. He loosened his hold at her neck and flipped up her nightgown, leaning over her close enough to brush his lips against her cheek. "You belong to me now, little Ana."

Reduced to a state of numb shock, she lay with tears burning in her eyes, their shimmer blurring the tangle of her red hair stretched across the bed linens. During the tussle, the rest of her coif had come down, and several sterling silver hair sticks were strewn over the bed.

The lantern light gleamed ominously over the sharp tip of one like an omen.

Or maybe even a sign from the Creator.

"I am not a possession!" she screamed while twisting her face to the side. After jerking the hair decoration free, Anastasia plunged it toward the offending part of her new husband.

She expected it to be in vain. He should have swept her hand away and taught her a lesson, but the lucky stab landed. The end speared through the flesh at the crease of his thigh, withdrew, and sank into another more sensitive location. For a moment, they were both shocked. She'd not only stabbed him, but she'd done it a second time.

Edward's warm blood gushed over her fingers to the rhythm of his heartbeat. Spurt-spurt, spurt-spurt. Her belly lurched upward, and bile rose into her mouth.

"You whore!"

The prince backhanded her, snapping Ana's head back.

VIVIENNE SAVAGE

Pain exploded over the left side of her face, and her cheek bloomed with heat, but with one hand cupping his groin and the other flailing to catch her wrist, Edward remained at a disadvantage. His efforts to staunch his own blood flow made it difficult to fight her away effectively.

Tears had half blinded Anastasia, reducing her strikes to a wild series of stabs toward his body without looking, seeing, or caring where she pierced him. None of it mattered as long as the hateful bastard was hurting too much to hit her again.

She struck his chest, and the hairpin sank through the cloth. A crimson stain bloomed across the breast of his tunic. He wheezed and collapsed to the bed when she finally scurried away.

The princess stared at Edward's twitching body and knew she needed to escape before the guards returned to their posts. Away to where? She didn't know, but she shuddered at the thought of what they would find once they realized her victim was missing.

She'd be named a murderer.

They'd hang her for this.

No, such punishment was saved for the common rabble and military deserters. She'd be walled inside a tower to receive her meals through a tiny slot for the rest of her life. She'd never see the open blue skies again.

While Prince Edward lay dying in her bed, she stripped away the blood-soaked night rail and dressing gown then hurried to the wardrobe. With tears rolling down her cheeks, she tore open the wooden door to find the spacious closet lined with frilly dresses and extravagant gowns.

It took her less than a minute to stuff a few chemises and tunics into one of her favorite, oversized carpet bags, and even less time to squeeze into a pair of riding breeches. Time wasn't on her side, but she couldn't bear to leave empty-handed.

While princesses weren't traditionally trained in the art of combat, she armed herself with the only weapon she could confidently wield — a fully charged magic wand gifted at the time of her birth. She ran her fingers over the gift from a fairy grandmother she'd never met, the thin shaft of ivory sleek, polished, and perfect.

Her father had allowed her to keep it for one reason, because she had truly promised to stop eating until he'd turned it over to her.

In fresh, unbloodied clothes, Anastasia rushed from the bedroom and hurried down the servants' staircase into their quarters.

Once outside, she had one destination: the stables. Sterling had been among the many belongings moved from her former home. She tiptoed past a sleeping groom sitting on the ground beside the doors. The young man's cap had been pulled over his face, a flagon of dark, foamy beer half-finished between his knees.

Without disturbing him, she entered the barn and found curious faces watching her in passing. A golden palomino nickered in greeting, the animal a gift from royal relatives

VIVIENNE SAVAGE

abroad. She didn't want him.

Of course, the black beauties owned by her parents weren't among the equine faces peeking at her from the stalls.

Edward hadn't lied. Her father and mother had truly abandoned her with no plans of remaining for the wedding. Her brows furrowed. Had it been his intention all along to be rid of her? Had something happened to her mother?

Tears blurred her vision, so she pushed the questions aside and focused on escape. If she fell apart now, they'd catch her and bring her back.

She found Sterling pacing nervously within a spacious stall at the end of the row and spent the first few moments of their reunion with her arms around the mare's neck. Sterling didn't make any judgments. She nickered gently and pressed her furry cheek against Anastasia's face.

"I love you," she whispered to her four-legged friend, breathing in the scent of fresh hay, grain, and the odors associated with livestock. After she saddled up and attached her small luggage bag, she led the mare outside past the sleeping stable boy, her heart began to slam in her chest anew. The kid's hat had fallen off, but he remained dead to the world and unaware of his surroundings.

They'd fire him for letting her slide past, if they didn't flog him. The poor boy. Ignoring the tight fist around her heart, Anastasia led Sterling from the stable, pausing once to hide in the shadows of the building when she heard a servant girl giggling in the dark with her footman suitor.

As she tiptoed away from her would-be husband's cooling corpse, two lovers happily prepared to do the very deed Edward had nearly forced upon her. When another sob threatened to come from her lips, Sterling touched her velvety soft nose to Ana's cheek, as if to say, "Shhh, it's going to be okay."

Grim determination flashed through the princess, restoring the steel to her spine. Edward hadn't broken her in the bedroom, and he wouldn't now, not when escape loomed within reach.

Once the lovers passed by, she climbed into the saddle and hurried away. She'd only have seconds between the patrol rounds to make her way to freedom. The castle squatted atop the hill, overlooking an enormous city nestled in the valley on one side and a messy swamp with coarse thickets and watery paths on the other. Her path to freedom lay to the north and through the swamp where she hoped the water would disguise their tracks.

The wand had enough of a charge for three intermediate spells. With the first, she circled the tool above her head in an elegant circle then thrust it downward toward Sterling's feet.

Most advanced sorceresses and wizards could cast the haste spell without a wand or staff, hastening the speed of travel by cutting a journey from tedious days to mere hours. The enchantment was a well-known, expensive piece of magic.

"Let's go home, girl."

For most of the night, she and Sterling were a silver breeze skirting over the wild plains beyond the swampland. They had slipped through checkpoints manned by drowsy guardsmen and onto the open highway stretched between the borders of Dalborough and Creag Morden.

By sunrise, both the spell and Anastasia's stamina had faded, but she was no longer in the kingdom. The tenacious princess hung in the saddle, slouched drowsily over Sterling's neck. A fork in the road labeled by two signs told her the way to their capital city of Lorehaven was north. The second path, a narrow road parallel to the Forest of the Ghost Winds, turned sharply east and cut through the forest.

The corner of Anastasia's mouth twitched. Mothers and fathers of Creag Morden whispered nighttime stories to their offspring about terrifying hags who boiled children into candy and chopped unfortunate wanderers into potion ingredients. Supposedly, their spirits walked the woods for eternity seeking justice.

"I don't think we'll be going that way, will we, Sterling?" she asked the mare, suddenly cured of her lethargy. She sat upright again in the saddle. "Shortcut or no, I'd rather take the safer road."

She turned the mare to the left fork and continued onward. The longer trip wouldn't be so bad, she figured, and allowed her time to think, to plan what she would say when she returned home.

If she'd remained behind at Darkmoor Castle, if she'd let Edward have his way, she'd be awakening to breakfast in bed, preparing to become a blushing bride.

Instead, she'd listened to her pride. And didn't regret her choice at all.

With her second wind regained, she nudged Sterling into a trot. The surroundings became familiar, a narrow road dividing the woods from the gentle, rolling hills to her left. In a day, she'd be home.

To the left, a three-story watchtower arose like a brick and mortar toothpick in an endless sea of grass. Beside it in a small, fenced-in pasture, three horses nibbled the sweet grass. Anastasia saw one watchguard drowsing at the southward facing post. His chin dipped toward his armored chest, then he stilled altogether. As she passed by the empty window overlooking the road and forest, her belly twisted with stress.

Why am I so afraid of them seeing me? she wondered.

Word of Edward's murder couldn't have traveled so far, could it? Aside from that, travelers frequently moved along the roads, and her behavior was nothing unusual.

"There she is!" a voice cried.

Anastasia started and twisted in the saddle to stare at the tower with wide eyes. The missing soldier from the second level had leaned out of the window to point. "The princess is here! Sound the alarm!"

Her expected arrival could only mean Darkmoor's magician, Rangvald, had sent word ahead via magical means. Another shout echoed across the brightening sky and two guards rushed from the tower to leap astride their horses.

A third descended from the tower's lookout point, sitting astride the back of a massive griffin. The animal wore spurs on its avian forelegs and looked like it meant business.

What had they been told about her to come out with the Griffin Guard? A few dozen scenarios flashed through her mind of bribed guards dragging her to certain death in Dalborough.

"Halt, Princess!" one of the horse-riders called.

To hell with that. She tapped her heel against Sterling's ribs and the lean mare shot off like a thunderbolt. When she risked a glance over her shoulder to see the trio closing in, she saw the griffin in the lead, each powerful whoosh of his wings bringing him yards closer and drowning out the bass of Sterling's unshod hooves beating the ground.

Anastasia veered to the right and burst into the tree line, branches scratching her face and upper chest. She leaned forward close to Sterling's neck and dropped her fingers to the wand. Two charges left. With two charges, she could obliterate them, or tax Sterling even further with another haste spell. The latter would jeopardize her mare's life.

As she stroked her thumb over the polished weapon and contemplated defensive measures, the ground quaked and shook. Anastasia looked to their rear to see the forest closing in behind her and great branches merging together to form a net. The griffin rider had already surrendered the chase, his wingspan too broad to soar through the forest. While they were elegant forces to be feared in aerial combat, griffins had no place racing on the ground.

"We're losing them!" a man cried.

"What the—?" one of the men's voices called. His horse neighed and the pursuit ended as the forest abruptly slammed shut behind her, the trunks of many closely positioned trees creating a sturdier barricade than the gates enclosing her father's castle. The forest had shielded her.

Or trapped her. It was too early for Anastasia to determine which.

The terror-inducing chase had depleted all of her oxygen, making the air whistle in and out of her chest. She slumped over the pommel of the saddle and, as they slowed to a walk, Anastasia quickly gasped to fill her starving lungs. The rich, earthy scent of the shaded path greeted her, its air cool and moist compared to the dry sun beyond. Hair clung against her perspiring brow and her heart slammed against her ribs, a relentless drumbeat pulsing in her ears.

She wasn't as capable a rider as her father, and the mad gallop across the plains had taxed her and Sterling to the limit. The mare nervously shifted in place, snorting and flaring her nostrils when her rider nudged her to go on. With some coaxing, she continued down a narrow path of packed earth between the trees.

They walked for hours while searching for an outlet from the forest, subject to the persistent sensation of eyes watching from the shadowed bushes. The thick canopy above them concealed the direction of the sun and dashed any hopes of

VIVIENNE SAVAGE

determining the direction. Occasionally, she heard a sound to her left or right, but when she whipped around to face the source of the noise, she saw nothing.

"Ghost winds, silly. There's nothing to fear," she told herself while dismounting. "This forest isn't named the Ghost Winds for nothing." She inhaled a deep breath, pushed her shoulders back, and walked with her chin raised and a hand on Sterling's reins.

"So much for returning to the castle before dark…. I think we're going in circles," she said a while later while shivering. As the thought came to her mind, the unforgiving wind picked up, its bitter chill felt down to the core of Ana's bones. "So cold." She'd been stubborn about relying on the wand to find her way out of the woods, but hunger tempted her to draw it one more time.

It would be worth spending another charge to summon a compass, or even a will-o'-wisp to lead her home.

But rest would be even better.

"Are you lost, little girl?" a woman's voice spoke up from her rear, so soft it was nearly lost in the biting wind whipping against Anastasia's face.

Ana spun around and stared at a fragile figure in a dark blue cloak. Stringy gray hair spilled from the woman's hood, framing a wrinkled face with rosy cheeks. The woman's cloudy gray eyes could have been beautiful once. Now they were only intriguing, blind but not unseeing.

"Who are you?" Anastasia asked uncertainly. She hung

back and kept her distance.

"An old woman. Only an old woman," the hag said. Her semi-toothless smile eased Anastasia's heart, bringing a strange sense of comfort. "An old woman with a spare bed and a pot of delicious dinner to share. Shall you come with me, lovely?"

While she'd been warned about hags in forests with pots of suspicious dinners, she had few other alternatives. She could wander the forest until she died from exposure, risk capture by corrupt soldiers who would no doubt accept a large purse for her return to Dalborough, or test her luck against the hag and be boiled in the same pot as dinner.

"Do you live nearby?"

The woman's grandmotherly smile never faded. "Yes, dearie. I do. Come along now."

Hadn't her father always told her never to trust strangers?

He'd also promptly sold her into marriage to one, too. The thought struck her as bittersweet irony that the man she'd trusted more than anything had betrayed her so completely when it counted most.

"I have lodgings for your beautiful friend. Wouldn't she love some grain and oats with sweet molasses?"

Sterling nickered in apparent agreement.

"We are both starved, yes," Anastasia agreed. She pursed her lips thoughtfully. "Are you a forest witch?"

"Witch? Hardly," the old woman said. "Only a lonely grandmother wishing for an evening's company. Now come,

VIVIENNE SAVAGE

before you both catch your death of cold."

Although Anastasia had wandered the woods lost and alone for hours, they reached the hag's cottage in mere minutes, making her wonder how she had missed stumbling upon it, or even catching sight of it between the trees. She had to be blind and senseless.

A delicious aroma greeted her as she stepped into the clearing, like a cloud of cinnamon and sugar floated above the home instead of the open skies.

The house itself was built from stone and wood, its tiled roof bright red and glossy beneath the dusky sky. A few stars twinkled at the edge of the horizon above the trees rising on the meadow's perimeter. There were even three husky, pristine white cows grazing amidst the waist-high grass beside a single golden bull. They watched Anastasia with disinterested blue eyes.

"My name is Eleanor, and you are welcome to my home. Release your horse here to graze, if you wish. My cows will cause her no harm."

The silver mare practically danced a jig when the saddle came down from her back. She bolted into the field without a second glance.

Despite the warm welcome, Anastasia lingered at the threshold without entering. She'd heard tales of witches luring the innocent into their cabins to devour them in stews and pastries. "You're more than a lonely grandmother. I can *feel* the magic here," she said warily.

Out of the oven and into the frying pan. It would be Ana's luck to escape a would-be rapist and end up in some hag's stew pot.

"Such a clever girl. Indeed, I am."

"Is it too much to ask for a vow of safety?"

"Far from it." Eleanor flashed another toothless grin. "No harm shall come to you by my hand or words. I swear on my own power and mother's grave, what I do for you now is in kindness without debt incurred or obligation made."

"Thank you," Anastasia said appreciatively, a little abashed about asking in the first place. Maybe it appeared rude of her, but it was only another part of life when entering the abode of sorceresses and witches. After escaping one kind of slavery, she'd do anything to avoid entering another.

"I'm sorry," she apologized. "I've had a difficult day. I mean no insult."

Another glance behind her back revealed Sterling drinking clear-running water from a spring at the edge of the flowers. As she entered the cottage, a familiar tingle ran down her spine and spread to the tips of her fingers. Her skin warmed, and the aching in her feet diminished.

Any place touched by human emotion and life had a spirit. Forests, manors, hilltops, deserts, and even valleys. But the most powerful spirits were the ones who inhabited a home. Home Sweet Home was the most basic of spells, a charm which came naturally once the soul of a residence accepted its occupant or even a cherished guest, but she'd

VIVIENNE SAVAGE

never experienced it outside of her father's palace. She hadn't even felt it when she entered Edward's castle, as if the cold stone and mortar had loathed her as much as he did.

"Have a seat, little one," Eleanor said. She gestured toward a chair at a small wooden table set for two with a pair of steaming mugs.

"Were you expecting me?"

"I'm old, dearie. I've dealt in magic for a very long time, and while I knew you were coming one evening, I couldn't pinpoint when…." Eleanor trailed to gaze out a window.

"That makes you a seer."

Eleanor chuckled. "I only dabble in it as a hobby, and nothing more." When Ana raised one brow in a questioning look, the old woman continued, "I prefer other magical tools and talents over the art of anticipating the future. Shall you have bread with your stew?"

Anastasia's belly burbled, demanding a full meal after a long night and day of riding and an even longer evening wandering in circles. "Yes, please."

"Excellent! Sit tight."

The old woman hustled to the bubbling cauldron where a savory soup filled the cottage's air with the aroma of veggies and herbs. She ladled a large serving into a bowl and set it in front of her guest before taking the opposite seat with a smaller portion in her bowl.

Initially, Anastasia picked at her meal with delicate spoonfuls and sips, demonstrating court decorum and the elegance expected of a princess. The tender cuts of meat tasted like rabbit, accompanied by hearty root vegetables and flavorful spices.

No meal had ever tasted so fine.

Eleanor squinted at her with her cloudy gray eyes. "There are no members of royalty here," she said with a quiet smile. "I won't judge."

Anastasia hesitated. "It's quite good," she assured the hag. Her gaze returned to the stew; then she began shoveling food into her mouth and tearing pieces of bread to dip into the broth.

"Have you run away from home?"

A little broth went down the wrong pipe. Ana sputtered and coughed until she righted the problem, but even afterward, her eyes watered and her face felt hot. "Why would you ask that?"

"It isn't common for a young woman such as yourself to come along this way. No traveler enters the Ghost Winds."

"Then why do you live here?"

"The peace, of course. Do you see any militiamen skulking around with their gunpowder weapons? Members of the royal guard? City watchman lurking by windows to take bribes?"

"No," Ana said. She raised the bowl to her lips and tipped it, pouring the tasty remnants into her mouth.

"Seconds?"

"Oh no, no thank you. I couldn't possibly eat another bite."

VIVIENNE SAVAGE

"Then how about a hot and relaxing bath?"

"As much as I would love to accept the offer—"

"Won't this fit you?" Eleanor asked. With previously empty hands, she presented Ana with a cotton shift patterned with lavender flowers. It smelled like sunshine, the fabric softer than anything she'd ever received from the royal tailors.

Eleanor wouldn't take no for an answer, insisting that the water was already prepared. So to the bath she went, after twisting her hair to the nape of her neck and pinning it in place. The high-backed, claw-foot tub smelled like medicine, and while she didn't know what the forest witch had poured in, she'd try anything to wash away the memory of Edward's filthy hands.

As she sank into the water, tears burned the corners of her eyes and spilled from behind her eyelids. A stranger in the woods had shown more compassion in an hour than her new in-laws had in the two days since their meeting.

Over an hour passed, but the water never lost a fraction of its warmth. She lingered until her skin wrinkled and the heat loosened her aching muscles.

By the time she crawled into bed, she could barely keep her eyes open to see the sheets she had drawn over her body.

Chapter 3

I N HER DREAMS, Ana walked amidst the flowers of a secret garden.

Marble statues surrounded her, each one more beautiful than the last. There were women dancing with men nearby in a circle while a band played. A celebration carried on around them, and cheerful party-goers smiled to her courteously.

"Good evening, Princess."

"A pleasure to meet you, Princess."

The air was sweet with the smell of fresh water and wild blossoms, and in the distance, she saw the sun on the horizon. It blazed gold above the forests beneath the mountain, and the sight stole her breath away.

This mountaintop castle struck her as more beautiful than anything she'd ever seen. She gazed around in wonder and meandered through a magical garden where pixies drifted through the air on butterfly wings, each one no larger than her hand. All aglow with magical light, they flitted around her.

In the rear garden, she noticed a solitary figure beside the decorative hedges. What had to be the most handsome man she would ever see in all of her life admired the twilight purple roses growing wild and untamed over a trellis beside the hedge maze. His profile revealed a strong nose and square jaw, framed by tresses redder than silken fire.

As if sensing her arrival, he turned to face her. He wore no shirt, revealing the brawny expanse of his chest, sparsely dusted with copper hair, but otherwise smooth and defined with powerful muscle. As was common among the savage barbarians of the east, he wore a strange garment from his waist to his knees, belted in place by thick leather. The green-patterned tartan hung low to reveal a line of muscular indentation on each side of his hips.

Ana wanted to trace her fingers there. He was hard and sinewy in all the right places. Heat rushed to her cheeks, shame urging her to forget any intention of fondly touching this man, this dream stranger.

But if it is a dream, may I not touch him and do as I will? Who would know but me?

As she offered a gloved hand to him, he bowed low and kissed the back of her knuckles. "Good day to you, my lady."

"Good day, my lord. If you don't mind my asking, where are we?"

When he smiled, his eyes twinkled with mirth, and her lungs ceased to cooperate. "In my garden, of course. And you're my special guest of the evening."

"But I was not aware of an invitation to become anyone's special guest."

"That is most peculiar. Are you not my princess, lass?" the young man asked. His voice was soft, a contrast to the rugged angles of his face and the body hardened by battle.

Red. She'd always been fascinated with red-haired men, though they were disliked in her kingdom. Red indicated heathen blood, a trait inherited from those related to the savages east of the mountain.

She had one as an ancestor many generations back, though she was the first child in two centuries to inherit their ginger coloring.

"Your princess?" she questioned.

"Aye. Are you not mine?"

She couldn't be his princess, could she? While she knew it was a dream, she couldn't bring herself to lie. After a quick shake of her head, she stepped forward again toward him and became aware of her dress. She wore her favorite, a gown in copper and black with multiple layers of glossy fabric and golden underskirts. The neckline shirred her shoulders and revealed a generous amount of décolletage. She'd loved the gown from the second she saw it in the dressmaker's shop, especially since the seamstress had admitted she designed the outfit with Anastasia in mind.

"I don't believe I am," Anastasia said sadly. "I am Princess Anastasia of Creag Morden, but I belong to no one."

"If you are not my princess, would you be willing to become mine?"

"My lord, I hardly know you."

"Will you come to know me then?" he asked.

Anastasia startled awake at noon, baffled to discover the

morning had passed her by. She never slept in at the castle. She stared at the swinging pendulum dangling from a cuckoo clock on the wall. The little bird popped out, tweeted, retreated, and bounced out again on its perch. After its twelfth chirp, it sang a song as sweet as the music from the morning finches outside her former bedroom window.

Definitely enchanted.

Although the clock had no way of knowing what it had done, she loathed it for interrupting her reply to the literal fantasy man of her dreams.

"Yes," she murmured to the air. "You could court me. If only you were real."

With a quiet sigh, she examined her surroundings and rose from the bed.

Nearby, a neatly folded pair of leggings, tunic, and a traveler's cloak awaited her. The clothes from her bag smelled as delightful as her loaned nightgown did, as if sunshine infused them. She tugged on the fresh outfit and shambled out of the bedroom to find the old lady humming from a rocking chair on the porch. Her knitting needles glinted in the afternoon sun.

"Good day, my dear."

"Good day," Ana murmured back.

"Your mare has some spirit in her, and she's quite rested and ready to undertake the rest of your journey, but I have a word of advice for you, dear girl."

"Advice?"

"Yes. Plenty. You will have an urgent choice to make, Anastasia Rose. This choice will affect thousands, and its consequences shall ripple across the lands from one kingdom to the next."

Anastasia stared at the witch, flabbergasted. "Me? I have an urgent choice to make? Why me?"

"Because you are you, of course," the old woman stated. "Twice, you will be tested, and each time, you will have only one chance."

"What must I do?"

"I cannot tell you. But when the time comes, you'll feel it," Eleanor said, raising one hand to touch Ana above her heart, "here. Now come and have these muffins. I'll pack several for your journey."

As Anastasia devoured one of the berry muffins, the snaggle-toothed old woman prepared a small basket with several more and a fat peach from one of her trees. She nestled a bottle of fresh milk alongside them.

Overcome with gratitude, Ana threw her arms around the old lady. "Thank you. From the bottom of my heart, thank you for all that you've done."

"Think nothing of it, dearie."

"Can't you tell me more about this choice?"

"I've already said more than I should. Go and travel with care, but remember my warning." The cryptic old woman smiled fondly and kissed her cheek. "You are stronger than you believe."

VIVIENNE SAVAGE

Daunted by the gravity of the woman's prophecy, Anastasia nodded. "Thank you again for taking me in. And thank you for your warning."

After mounting her horse, Ana watched Eleanor step into her little cottage and shut the door. She nudged Sterling toward the path and set out for the long walk home. This time, she had no trouble finding her way through the forest. The mist had subsided, and the canopy above appeared thinner, allowing sunlight to filter between the branches. She felt its warmth on her face and smiled.

If she couldn't return to the castle, at the very least, she thought the king would supply her with enough money to cross the sea. She'd take an ocean voyage to one of their kingdom's allies and start a new life for herself as a commoner.

I can do it, Ana told herself while loosening the white-knuckled grip on the reins. A difficult life as a commoner beat a privileged life as a slave. Her father wouldn't doom her to imprisonment. He loved her that much, didn't he?

Would knights and guardsmen from Dalborough await her at the castle, ready to nab the runaway princess and discipline her for crimes against the crown? With two charges remaining on the magic wand, she wouldn't go back without a fight.

In his dreams, Alistair was human again.

He'd had fingers and toes, the ability to walk on two

strong legs, and a voice that didn't rumble on the edge of a growl. He'd been human, and there had been a princess of such breathtaking beauty he'd been struck dumb at the sight of her. And when she spoke to him, he couldn't help but ask if she was his.

When he awakened on the top of the tower in the cool air, awareness of his oversized limbs and serpentine tail reminded him of the truth. He stretched one immense foreleg and curled his claws over stone. The wind buffeted against the thick membrane of his scaled wings.

He wasn't a human man again after all.

Almost thirteen years had passed since the fairy cursed him to live as only a beast, unable to shift from his dragon body to the two-legged form of a man again. In this massive state, he could no longer visit most rooms of the castle where he had been raised, and wherever he traveled outside of Cairn Ocland, he was feared and loathed as a monster.

Cairn Ocland, the kingdom his family had nourished for centuries, was all but destroyed. The enemy had raided the villages, scattered its people, and afflicted the earth they once worshipped under a curse so dark no druid could grow a single bean in its soil.

Why couldn't he have died with his parents, fighting for the kingdom they'd loved so much?

At the time, he'd been a young man of eighteen, ignorant and hurting when he emerged from the castle cellar to find a wasteland on their mountain peak. Soldiers from Dalborough

VIVIENNE SAVAGE

had razed their orchards, slaughtered their livestock, and killed the magnificent Witch Queen Liadh. He found his mother's corpse at the edge of the mountain overlooking the countryside below. She'd fought to the very end.

His father's ashes weren't far from her. While the people of Cairn Ocland knew him as the Dragon King Rua, people to the west knew him only as the witch's monstrous mount and bodyguard. Their ways were held sacred and secret, the truth of his ability to shapeshift taken to the grave.

Along with the knowledge of their son. At the onset of the battle, his mother had enchanted him beneath a powerful sleeping spell and hidden him in the castle before concealing it beneath a magical barrier.

At first, he mourned, and as time went by, he grew bitter and angry. And in his brief, as well as childish rage, he'd done the unforgivable by taking his fury out on others who were innocent. But he didn't deserve this awful curse. He didn't deserve to have his humanity stripped from him.

"If thou wish to behave like a beast, then a beast thou shall be." The fairy's words rang through his memory, imperious and undeniable.

Until I find a true love to see the human in me.

Could he find any woman willing to love him when all she saw was teeth and enormous claws? Alistair had his doubts. Women wanted a beautiful prince in shining armor, or so claimed the tales his mother once told him. Those stories never featured a prince in shining scales.

His dream troubled him long after he awakened to endure another day of his lonely existence.

What he wouldn't give for a book to read, but he couldn't hold one between his large claws. Could he even remember how to read or would the words swim together in a mystifying jumble of letters?

Alistair sighed.

Time blurred, each day the same, but hours after his awakening, he realized something was amiss with his surroundings. He had descended the tower to eat, but when he returned to the castle grounds, he smelled the unmistakable, familiar scent of human perspiration. Oily notes of fear and anxiety reached his nose.

The king had sent another mercenary to steal from Alistair's garden. The realization swept him into a rage and sent him bounding down the abandoned path. He sprang into the garden but found only the lingering smell of an intruder. His eyes picked up nothing.

Alistair growled. He hurried to the wall of purple dusk roses and investigated them thoroughly. Unharmed. The last group the king sent had maimed them so thoroughly he'd been afraid they would never grow back. While the castle's enchantment seemed thrilled to rejuvenate the orchards and regenerate the structures on the grounds, it had never meddled with his mother's beloved, strange flowers.

Perhaps it was because they too were magical, and magic conflicted with magic?

VIVIENNE SAVAGE

He glanced around again. His spine tingled from his nape to the tip of his tail. He didn't feel alone.

He sniffed, and the smell of perspiration worsened, the source of it nearby. He growled and swung around again while following the smell.

No one. He saw no one. The garden was wide and open, its paths made from circular stepping stones decorated with garnet chips arranged in the pattern of fairies. Several marble benches occupied the edge of the vast space. A fountain featuring a statue of a woman in dance occupied the center. She held a pitcher in one outstretched hand, and from it, water poured in a stream toward the pool around her feet.

His mother had loved this place, and it incensed him to smell a stranger among her most cherished belongings.

Growling, he twisted around to search behind him, seeing movement from the corner of his eye. As he did, a flask arced through the air and crashed against the stone beside his right foreleg. Alistair glanced down at it. Steam arose from the puddle of dark substance; then his next breath caught in his lungs. He couldn't breathe. The steam created a choking fog and strangled him.

Dragon's bane!

He knew of its existence but thought only the people of the distant Liang knew how to create the foul concoction. His mother claimed the difficult alchemical process limited the number of people capable of creating it. His father had warned him of its highly toxic effect to their kind.

Bounding forward to escape the smog cloud, he searched the area for the source. His eyes burned, and tears blurred his vision, the pain indescribable. A quick figure darted across the path; then a storm of blades cut through the air. Alistair arched in pain, giving a soundless roar.

The king had sent another assassin.

Another blade struck him from the right. Before he could whirl and snap his jaws, the thief vanished and appeared to the left. He jabbed forward with his deadly sword, slicing easily through Alistair's tough hide.

Also enchanted.

Following his instinct, he whipped with his tail in a wide arc, catching the killer-for-hire as he materialized again. It was a lucky hit. The man's sword skittered away over the stone. The assassin sucked in his breath and somersaulted backward, and in the blink of an eye, vanished into smoke again.

Breathe. Breathe. I must get it out, Alistair told himself. The toxin was lodged in his lungs, as if it were more than poisonous smoke. His chest shuddered from the exertion and his ribs ached. A stream of smoke left his nostrils, a fraction of what he'd taken in.

Like most dragons, he could hold his breath for an extraordinary amount of time. For nearly ten minutes. Sometimes fifteen on a good lung of air. While he had no fear of suffocating, the object of the poison had been designed to do something else.

If he couldn't exhale the air trapped in his lungs, he

couldn't breathe fire to defend himself. He could take flight and escape, but the act of flying would burn rapidly through his air reserve. He'd suffocate and plummet from the sky.

No. I won't lose to him. Not now.

The human was close, confident but not unafraid. Alistair took control of his own senses, though the smell of his opponent surrounded him. It was everywhere at once. A cut to his back, a slice to his wing, a jab at his belly that his scales deflected. He swiped with his claw, but the agile man deflected it.

Back and forth across the stone paths they battled, claws and steel, tooth and magic. A bolt sizzled from the man's gloved palm where an enchanted crystal contained the spell for electricity.

The magical lance sparked across Alistair's snout, blinding and painful. His eyes closed instinctively, and within seconds, he was under siege again by the next attack.

He had to fight and push through the pain. His lungs seized again, but with another cough, he heaved out the toxin.

Sweet air filled Alistair's lungs.

They continued to battle, and a lucky blow caught the assassin's side with one talon, ripping through his protective armor. The man fumbled for another flask from a line of three in a row on a leather bandolier. He threw it down on the ground, but before it could shatter, Alistair spread his wings and swept them down. He launched his body into the clean air and avoided the fog.

His assailant vanished, realizing his missed opportunity might cost him his life.

"Coward!" Alistair roared. He sucked in another breath of clean air, letting it fill his lungs and expand his chest. His jaws opened, and a wave of fire flashed from his gaping maw. He swept it to each side, incinerating plant life in the process.

The assassin cried out, startled by an indirect hit. The substance of a dragon's breath weapon wasn't mere fire. It clung to skin like a flammable fuel. Screaming, he brushed it from his armor and streaked toward the edge of the courtyard. He moved quickly, but not quicker than a dragon in the air.

No, you don't, Alistair thought. He swooped down and exhaled another breath. This time, the full force of his fury struck his target.

The nameless warrior from Liang threw up a spell wall, but the onslaught of heat vaporized it, and the resplendent, magical barrier collapsed. Moments later, nothing remained but ashen bones.

Alistair collapsed to the smoldering ground and gasped for breath. His entire chest ached, and every inch of his body hurt. Hours passed while he lay ravaged by pain, and when he was finally able to move again, rage took the place of his agony.

No longer would he allow the king to send thieves, knights, and alchemists. For the first time since their war began, he'd felt close to losing his life.

Alistair turned to the northwest and stared at the distant horizon.

No more.

Today, he would seek the king and teach him what happened to men who meddled with dragons.

By evening, she was once again on the path to Lorehaven. She nibbled one of the muffins Eleanor had packed in the satchel and stopped once to allow Sterling to graze from the knee-high summer grass beside the road.

She was stalling. Fear made it easy to drag her feet, so to speak, but she pulled her hood up and sniffed the air. A peculiar smell reached her, and it only intensified as she traveled the road leading to the city's southern gate.

But her suspicion wasn't confirmed until Lorehaven sounded the alarm. Shrill bells tolled, screaming for citizens to take refuge in the pre-appointed safe havens.

It wasn't a drill. The dragon had returned again.

She saw him approaching from a few miles east of the city and moving fast. The tiny, scarlet speck in the distance grew larger until Anastasia distinguished the outline of two enormous wings. Dark, black smoke billowed toward the sky, rising from the scorched remnants of the guard post outside the city.

A sinking, heavy feeling at the pit of her stomach told her where the dragon was headed.

"Hurry!" she urged Sterling as they raced for the city gate.

The watchman stationed at the nearby tower appeared

as startled to see a lone rider as he did to see the dragon approaching the city from the east. He screamed down to someone below, and the gates rolled open.

They must have thought her to be a terrified traveler hoping to find safety in the city. She didn't stop to answer questions when she burst past them en route to the castle despite their cries for her to halt.

Above them, a shadow passed over Lorehaven, its long tail stretching behind it like a kite's ribbon.

Not an it. A he, she decided. The dragon's breadth of figure and build struck her as masculine, a majestic creature as brilliant as the rubies decorating her favorite tiara.

She watched him soar, her emotions treading a fine line between awe and envy. In their panic, the townspeople had vacated the roads, and it struck her as sad that they had nowhere else to go and sought refuge from a fire-breathing beast in wooden cottages.

No guards awaited her at the gates, but the grounds had been reduced to bedlam. As she rode through, startled faces filled with recognition and called out to her.

"Princess?" asked a guard who crossed her path.

"Where is my father?"

Every protective spell had been activated. Magic sizzled in the air, creating a hurricane of charms in every defensive variety.

"In the courtyard," the soldier replied. "The dragon has landed, your majesty. You must not go that way. Let me lead

VIVIENNE SAVAGE

you to safe—"

"No!" She jerked the reins to the left when he reached to take them from her. Sterling dashed around him and charged into the courtyard.

Her father, protected by a suit of golden armor, faced off against the dragon. Flames licked the tops of the ornamental trees, their burning boughs sending up plumes of smoke toward the heavens.

"Father!"

"Anastasia?" King Morgan's eyes widened in alarm. "Seek safety, child! Head to the lowest level of the castle and evacuate through the tunnels!"

A member of the royal guard touched her arm, meaning to drag her aside. She jerked away instead.

Is this what Eleanor referred to? My choice? Am I meant to speak with this dragon? she wondered.

"No! I won't run and hide again!" She darted forward to her father's side, magic wand in hand to shield them both.

The dragon recoiled as if her presence had frightened it. His eyes grew large, and the ridges above his brows raised over his reptilian face. The breath he had inhaled came out of him harmlessly without fire.

"Listen to me, Ana. I may never have this chance to speak with you again. Know that I love you dearly, and acted in your best interests to keep you safe. Your mother and the rest of the staff have evacuated. Go to them now and save yourself. A carriage has been prepared, as of yesterday evening, waiting to take you away to safety."

Anastasia trembled. Dalborough had been in contact with him. He knew, and he'd taken steps to spirit her away somewhere. To protect her.

"What a touching reunion," the dragon rumbled in a deep voice, his chuckle reminding her of boulders tumbling down a mountain. Anastasia saw her own face reflected in his dinner-plate-sized eyes, their irises the ochre color of butterscotch fresh from the candy maker.

"This is between you and me, beast," King Morgan said.

"Indeed, it is. You will make a fine pet, human. Many times I have warned you, yet I remain dissatisfied. Your futile efforts to raid my mountain have ended in failure once more."

King Morgan stared down the great dragon in front of him. "I do not fear you, dragon." Compared to the enormous monster, his puny sword appeared to be only a thin shard of useless metal.

"Your panicked heart betrays your composure, proud king. How quickly would you lose it if your dear daughter danced in my flames? Shall we put it to the test?"

"No!" King Morgan cried. He threw himself between Ana and the monster. "Ana, run!"

Her father lunged forward and thrust with the blade toward the dragon's throat. Its enchantment flared, a flash of blue-white light exploding over the courtyard. It left shapes blinking in and out of her vision, and once it faded, she saw her father lying beneath the dragon's enormous claw, his broken blade shattered nearby on the cobblestone walking path.

"I should kill you for all you have done," the dragon hissed, "but death would be too easy for you. No. I will take you instead, pitiful king, to serve me for the remainder of your pathetic life."

"Leave my father alone!"

Her voice had power she hadn't known she possessed. The dragon flinched almost as if she'd struck him with magic instead. With a single, powerful backstroke from his wings, he jumped onto the stone wall to perch above them.

If she fled, the King and Queen of Dalborough would travel to the ends of Vale to demand justice for their son. Alternatively, if she remained in the palace, the two nations would be at war. Innocent citizens would suffer. It was no longer about her own freedom or the happiness of her parents.

With her eyes trained upon the dragon, Anastasia stepped toward him.

"Don't take my father. Take me instead," she offered.

"Ana!" The king struggled to sit up, but fell back with a wince, wrapping an arm around his chest. The armor had been crushed.

"You will give yourself in the place of your father to be my prisoner?"

"I will," she confirmed.

"Ana, do not do this," the king attempted to order her.

As her father's best men placed their lives between the monster and their king, Anastasia knew there could only be one choice.

She had to leave with the dragon and offer herself as the price for her kingdom's safety. Her father had taunted the creature, and in doing so, had doomed their kingdom.

"What will your choice be?" the dragon rumbled. He glowered at them from the ledge of a stone wall where it crouched precariously like the world's most enormous, reptilian bird. His wings fanned out alongside its body, scales covering them like thousands of ruby flecks with gilded edges.

There was a strange beauty to the dragon that had terrorized their city. An unexpected sense of majesty to the monster who her father both loathed and feared. Had she known it would be so handsome, she would have begged harder when beseeching the king to end his war against it.

Now it was much too late. Whether or not they lost their lives would come down to a single choice.

"I'll go with you," Ana said.

"Over my dead body," the king spat. "Kill the beast now while it stands before us."

At her father's command, archers raised bows and aimed arrows. Her father thought killing was the answer, but that wasn't to be the solution to their problem. Already, he'd sent so many hapless adventurers to their doom that the dragon no longer found his pitiful attempts amusing.

Would his archers succeed where so many had failed?

Anastasia raised her chin in an act of defiance. "No, Father. You gave me away to a terrible man. Now I have the right to give myself for a greater cause." She turned to face the dragon. "Make a promise now to cease setting fire to our kingdom's villages, and I will go with you happily, Dragon. May I have your word?"

The mighty beast chuckled. "Unlike humans who lie and deceive, I have never broken my word, beautiful princess."

She pursed her lips thoughtfully and glanced at her helpless father, who would no doubt surrender his life to rescue her from her fate if he could. In all of her life, she'd never seen him so vulnerable. "I want your word, an oath of blood bound in magic."

The dragon's nostrils flared, bright and piercing eyes growing wide.

"Is this acceptable to you, Sir Dragon?"

The tense wrinkle in the middle of the dragon's brow smoothed. "Sir Dragon. I like that. Aye, this is acceptable."

As fire raged around them from the tops of the trees to the palace gates at their rear, the king's guard waited on his command, their shields poised and swords ready. On his word, they would charge in to do combat against the monster.

But she would be caught in the middle.

Once the dragon abandoned the wall and settled back on his haunches, long tail writhing behind him on the stone ground, he tapped one black talon against the pad of his clawed hand.

"Your turn, Princess."

Anastasia held out her hand and closed her eyes. She felt

only pressure at first. When she opened her eyes, a fat droplet of blood had welled from the center of her palm. The tips of his talons were so sharp it took seconds for the pain to register.

"Don't do this, Ana," the king pleaded.

"It's for the best," she whispered. The moment of contact stung, a sizzling jolt sparking between them, unseen but felt by all standing within fifty meters. Two members of the palace guard jerked back and flinched, and another angled his body forward as if he meant to rush to her rescue.

"By dragon flame and heart's blood, my word is our bond. May the gods strike me from the sky if my vow is broken. Your life for their freedom, all within this kingdom shall be spared."

"My life is yours, Sir Dragon, from now and until my final breath, the price of freedom and life for all I hold dear. Unless challenged or threatened, you shall not harm any human or hurt my countrymen while I am yours."

His eyes flared red-orange, a glow like scorched coals in the dark. "Our vow is made."

"Our vow is made," she repeated.

As the deal was struck, her father wept out in horror.

"I love you, Papa. And I forgive you."

"Ana, please."

"It is done. Tell everyone I love them. Tell them I'm sorry. Tell them I'll miss them so much."

Warm, hard digits closed around her waist. An involuntary shudder ran through Ana's body, and then her feet were abruptly lifted from the ground. The wind pushed over her and through her hair, and as she opened her eyes, she saw the ground rushing away from her.

They were in flight.

The flaming guard towers became tiny red specks against the green surroundings. Without warning, an involuntary reaction came over her. Screaming, she beat at the dragon's clawed hand without success and gazed up into the inquisitive, scaled face of the beast.

"Put me down. Put me down!"

She'd known all along, deep down in her thoughts, that they would leave by air—but she also hadn't been prepared for the quick ascent into the sky. The dragon had his own haste spell, and with it, he'd shot into the clouds like a bullet from a flintlock pistol.

He laughed, the same grinding, rough noise at the back of his throat, a growl as much as it was a chuckle.

"Please!" My slaps bother him as much as a flea troubles a dog. Her palms ached by the time she stopped, bruised from the fruitless effort.

"Have you a desire for death?" the dragon asked. His voice was a deep rumble, a masculine brogue with a lyrical cadence.

Wouldn't the joke be on her if he turned out to be a she?

"N-no."

"Then stop. A fall from this height will be your death and no responsibility of mine," he grumbled.

"I'm afraid of heights!"

"Then close your eyes."

Of course, she had no hope of moving his clawed digits, even if the inclination remained. They were strong, each of the four easily as long as her forearm, and each talon may as well have been molded from steel.

"Where are you taking me?"

He didn't answer.

"Is this… this is the way to Benthwaite!" she cried above the noise generated by his flapping wings.

"Why ask our destination if you know the way?"

Although she couldn't be certain, Ana thought a hint of amusement colored the dragon's deep voice. The distance requiring days on horseback took a mere fraction of the time by dragon's wing. They rose higher into the skies until they breached the low-level clouds floating above the mountain range.

As her captor came in for a landing on the green plateau, she wondered how long they had flown. His claws sank into the soft earth, leaving deep gouges in the grass.

The moonlit view of the world below stole Ana's breath away—for the second time. She knew this mountain! A winding path illuminated by lanterns disappeared around the plateau, while the rest of the level road bisected an enormous courtyard with four neat rows of blossoming orange trees. Their wild fragrance filled the air, and together, they were more beautiful than the royal orchard.

Night had fallen, but darkness had been abolished by a

multitude of hanging lamps glowing down the cobbled path and high parapets. Lights shone in stained glass windows and lanterns gleamed near the castle doors, creating a marvelous spectacle.

The dragon lowered her gently to her feet on the ground. She stepped forward, too dazzled by her surroundings to make a prompt comment. A thousand questions whirled through her thoughts, and as her mind ran free, the dragon lowered to all fours and moved forward, his body sleek and muscular at once, an odd contrast of bulk and compact muscle.

Her captor led the way up the path, past the orange trees and a large fountain on the other side. The palace itself towered above them, an ominous and inviting presence of immense beauty. She couldn't believe her eyes that something so magnificent had been tucked away in the mountains all this time, occupied by only a dragon. Did dragons hire masons and laborers, or had he usurped the throne centuries ago from some lost and forgotten royal family?

"What am I to do now that I am here?" Ana asked, bewildered. "Are you keeping me like a hog for the slaughter?" she demanded.

Growling, the mighty beast whirled to face her, practically crashing his tail into the fountain. The spikes grazed the angelic statue crowning the center.

"Are you not Princess Anastasia of Creag Morden?" he demanded.

She started, taken aback by the recognition. She'd never

told him her name. "How did you…? I don't understand."

"Surprised that a dragon knows your name? Do you think me incapable of telling one human face from another?" Twin plumes of smoke and fire issued from both nostrils. She staggered back and bumped into a stone wall.

"No! That's not it!"

"Then. What. Is. It?" he asked, enunciating between each word.

A few hours ago, she'd been ready to embrace her demise, but she'd also never expected to literally stare death in its scaled, infuriated face either. As she dragged in a breath, a kind of foolish anger fell over Anastasia. She straightened her spine and stepped forward.

"Losing your temper over a few questions make you appear to be a very childish dragon, you should know. When I rode past Lorehaven, I saw you setting fire to the watch posts and I feared my family's palace would be next."

The beast stared at her, his unblinking amber-eyed gaze fixed to her face. At their close distance, almost nose to nose, she saw thin strands of green and gold against the amber, reminding Anastasia of a beautiful emerald and gold necklace her father once brought home from a trip abroad.

"It would have been," he answered in a lower tone. The anger and heat faded from his voice, and while it softened, the deep, rumbling noise remained. He dragged open the massive palace doors then ducked down to enter.

A relieved sigh escaped her when he moved away. Now

VIVIENNE SAVAGE

or never. She followed her captor into the castle, dreading what she would find.

Her jaw dropped.

The entrance hall stretched far above the dragon's head. They strode to the end of a wide corridor decorated with elaborate, hanging fixtures lit by glowing alchemical globes. Their pale golden light mimicked the sun, illuminating the treasures sparkling from nearby display cases.

Dragons loved treasure, so it shouldn't have surprised her. They reached a circular chamber beyond the hallway with a painted mural of angels stretched across its dome-shaped ceiling. No. Fairies, she realized, gazing at them in awe. Tiny sprites, flowers, and a lovely garden had been depicted above the dangling chandelier. It took her breath away.

This wasn't Darkmoor Castle. This place felt alive and loved, nurtured with care.

"This is beautiful." She bit her lower lip, wondering why a dragon needed so much extravagance and if he could appreciate the beauty and the majesty surrounding him.

He paused at the foot of the horseshoe-shaped stairs leading to the upper level. "Thank you."

"Did you build this palace?"

"No."

"Then how did you get it?"

Silence. The dragon continued to lead her to the upper floor, stony and refusing to acknowledge her question.

"Will you at least tell me your name?"

He stopped and turned to face her. "As far as I am concerned, the title of Beast shall suffice. It is what your father prefers."

Grasping for ways to make the best out of a bad situation, Ana smiled and said, "There, now we are properly introduced." She curtsied politely.

"So we are." Beast snorted, and the warm breath stirred her hair. "Do you believe you could be happy here, Princess Anastasia?"

Happiness is subjective, Ana thought. She'd been happy at home with her family, excluding her mother's frequent fits of insanity. Had Edward not been such a cruel bastard, she might have found happiness in Dalborough. Instead, she had faced a cruel fate. And now, here in this strange place, all she felt was relief that she had spared more bloodshed. "I could indeed have a pleasant life in this castle, and I'm quite happy to be here."

"You are pleased to be here?"

"Quite," she responded.

"What a strange woman you are."

"Do you intend to starve and beat me?" Or rape me? The question felt absurd the moment it passed through her mind. After all, he was a dragon. They were incompatible for the act, thankfully. Her cheeks flushed at the thought.

"No."

"Then I have little to fear and you have my gratitude. Thank you."

  VIVIENNE SAVAGE

"Heh." He turned away and continued down the carpeted hall. "You may visit any room and level of this castle, excluding the uppermost floor of the east wing."

"What is up there?"

The dragon rounded on her.

"Nothing you need to be concerned with," he snapped. "Is it so much, what I ask?"

"No, Beast, it's not. My apologies."

He huffed, bowed his head, and then resumed his sedate pace. "The dining room has sat empty. I am sure Hora will be pleased to see it used once more."

"Hora?"

"The palace matron," he answered over his shoulder. When her brows raised, he snorted. "Did you believe me to be the sole caretaker of this vast fortress?"

"But where are the others? I've seen no one since my arrival."

He gave another dry chuckle as he stopped at a small door, one of many with a standard-sized frame too small to accommodate his enormous size. He settled back, resembling a dog in his posture, and gestured with one of his claws. "Your bedchamber."

As her beating heart slammed a harsh rhythm against her ribs, Anastasia stepped forward and into the rest of her life.

No matter what, she couldn't allow herself to forget she was a prisoner, even if Beast's castle was better than the hell she'd left behind.

Chapter 4

As with everything else she'd seen so far, her room was beautiful. Three tall windows with stained glass arches provided a breathtaking view of the mountains. Even in the dead of night, they shone, lit silver by the full moon.

Heavy blue drapes hung around a large four-poster bed. Ana sat on the edge of the mattress and thought she had never felt anything softer. She ran her fingers over the luxurious, thick blanket then stood again and moved to inspect the hearth, where a small, cheery fire burned. More fairies decorated the mantle, carved into the gleaming wood amid lovingly depicted flowers and vines.

It's as if I was expected. Why else heat the room? she wondered.

"How do you like your bedchamber?"

Anastasia jerked around toward the source of the voice. A silver-haired woman stood in the doorway, wearing a bright smile on her slim, oval-shaped face. She'd arrived in silence, taking the princess completely by surprise.

"My apologies. I hadn't meant to startle you," she said. "When he told me you were becoming acquainted with your new room, I thought I would come to introduce myself. I am

Hora, matron of the castle."

"Oh! He spoke of you. Well, only briefly before he resumed a gruff attitude again and left. I didn't get to ask him a single thing about the rest of this place. Gone before I made it a few meters inside."

"Nothing unusual for him," Hora confirmed with a fond smile on her face. "I understand you came of your own free will in the place of the king. That makes you a very, very brave young woman."

"I had my reasons. It was... generous of him to allow me to come in my father's stead. The kingdom needs its king far more than it needs a princess."

And another war.

Hora watched her with a steel-gray gaze, her neutral expression unreadable. "I see," she said at last. "Well, Princess Anastasia, if you need anything, I am never far. It's easy to become lost in this large palace."

As the older woman drifted to the doorway, impulse forced a question to fly from Ana's lips. "Excuse me if I appear rude by asking, but where are the rest of the castle residents?"

"You and I are the only human souls in this castle," Hora said gently.

Ana startled at that revelation and glanced to the open doorway. No wonder the huge castle had seemed vacant and empty. Void of life. "Where is everyone?"

"The other servants are indisposed."

"So they weren't eaten?"

Hora shook her head, chuckling quietly. "No, dearest, he's never eaten a human. But enough of them, tell me, have you found everything to your liking? You didn't answer."

"It's a very lovely room," Ana replied. She moved to a wardrobe cabinet and opened it to reveal an array of dresses in different colors, styles, and fabrics. Silk, velvet, satin, and even the scandalous, thin cotton shifts that had come into fashion years ago in the southern provinces.

While she had admired the look from afar, she'd never had the courage to don one. Riding pants were one thing, but wiggling into a summer dress from Tournesol was beyond Ana's limits.

"I find there are many things to like," she continued while caressing the opulent fabric. Her fingers glided over the smooth material, and she imagined herself twirling across a ballroom floor with skirts swirling around her thighs. Her shoulders would be bare and her bosom heaving within the constraints of a corset, but she struggled to imagine the man guiding her in his arms. "But I wonder why he's shown me such kindness after promising tortures unknown to my father."

"Perhaps Beast has respect for bravery," the cheerful old woman countered.

"Was my father not brave to face him in our courtyard? Did he tell you that?"

"Was your father not the coward who sent assassins slithering into ours?"

Blast. Hora had her there.

VIVIENNE SAVAGE

"Just the same, I would show caution, dear one, and not look a gift horse in the mouth. I shall leave you to your exploration to resume my own household duties. Enjoy your room and all comforts it offers to you. Breakfast begins at eight each morning followed by lunch at noon. Tea is served at four and supper at eight. You may attend all or none of these meals at your own discretion, young princess."

"Whose clothes are these?"

Silence met her query. When Ana turned, she found the room empty. Once again, she was left alone to her own devices.

At first, she was content to explore the room, but she soon grew tired of her surroundings and emerged from the room to explore.

The remaining second-floor bedrooms were numerous, each one fancier than the next, though none held a candle to the chamber she'd been given by Beast. They were either too dark, too light, or at the wrong angle to receive the sun through their windows. Some smelled old and musty, and others felt cold and unloved.

She discovered a multi-story library nearby, spanning nearly thrice the breadth of her bedroom with an upper level accessible by ladder and a circular balcony. It could have easily held a grand ballroom, for it was so broad, its windows spacious, and the walls stretching toward a ceiling with a beautiful, golden-hued fresco.

Ana had never seen so many books gathered in one place outside of the academy. Her father's library would occupy a corner of this room, if that much. She climbed to the top and perused the highest shelves, finding a bounty in romantic classics, and then resumed her adventure.

No matter where she walked, there was no sign of Beast or Hora. No servants, no maids, no guardsman.

The castle appeared vacant of all life, a beautiful void shaped by the talented hands of skilled stonemasons and countless artists. She traveled halls filled with oil paintings depicting scenes of battle, noble life, and the pristine countryside of Cairn Ocland. She even found carved marble statues of great beauty in the light of windows or by balconies. The sculptor must have been fascinated by realism, having caught his subjects performing mundane duties such as polishing windows or sweeping floors.

Floor by floor, room by room, she explored her new home and found it as breathtaking as the castle she'd taken for granted in Creag Morden.

This new place was to be her home. And it was lonely.

With Beast's warning in mind, she remained clear of the castle's uppermost floor and suppressed her curiosity. Was this to be her life, surrounded by cold stone, lifeless beauty, and no company? She missed the garden at home filled with chipper birds and fat, sassy squirrels. She missed the maids and their gossip. She missed Victoria. How her friend must be frantic with worry.

Ana sighed.

She retraced her steps to the lower levels of the castle and approached the doors in the grand hall. She'd hoped to find Beast in the courtyard and ask him to discuss her new role in the castle; instead, she encountered the same empty space. She frowned.

"Nothing," she muttered out loud. "Not a single soul." Her brows creased as she circled an armored statue, standing tall and proud to the left of the door. She'd overlooked it when she first entered, but now, with a torch burning behind it, the statue was hard to miss. The firelight highlighted the intricate, lifelike details.

The former owners of the castle must have truly loved art.

Suppressing disappointment, she lifted her chin and returned to her room. Wearier than she'd ever been in all of her life, she crawled beneath the sheets, curled into a ball, and hugged a pillow close to her chest. Everything in her world had changed. In as little as two days, she'd gone from a reluctant princess bride to a murderer and a runaway, and now a dragon's prize.

Despite the exhaustion of the previous night, Anastasia awakened bright and early to the chirping of birds flitting in and out of the open window with a fresh, citrus-scented breeze. With the orange grove nearby in full bloom, she wondered if Beast would mind her visiting it to collect her own fruit.

She also wondered how she was to bathe. She ventured into the bathing room and found a high-backed, porcelain tub. It was beautiful, but it lacked the spigots attached to the tub she'd used in Darkmoor Castle, which had been attached to pipes constructed from dwarven craftsmanship.

She tried to imagine lugging her own buckets of water into the bathing room, and with grim determination, decided she had no other alternative. Perhaps she'd been stripped of all conveniences tied to her former life as a princess, but she refused to let it break her.

Tonight, she decided. Tonight she would find the kitchens and boil the water for her own bath. She would become strong.

In the meantime, she tidied her appearance. In the event that she crossed someone's path while searching the premises, she had to look her best, so she used the vanity table built from rich, golden brown oak awaiting her at the far wall with an assortment of brushes and grooming tools. She dragged one through her hair and bound it in a single plait before donning a plain, blue wool dress from the wardrobe in the dressing room.

It fit her curves as if tailor-made to her shape. She twirled in the mirror and watched it flare around her ankles with glee. It beat wearing a corset, and Ana's breasts were so small and modest she had no need of one anyway.

Satisfied with her appearance, Anastasia followed her nose to the first level where she stumbled upon an extravagant dining hall with a roaring fire crackling in the hearth. Despite being in the height of summer, the mountain peaks were chillier than the fertile valley of her birth. A familiar aroma

VIVIENNE SAVAGE

enticed her into a room and down the length of a massive table meant to entertain a huge number of guests, but set for only one.

"Allow me," a gruff voice said from another pair of entrance doors. There were two sets in all, each wide enough for Beast to step through. His massive draconic body approached the table, and with one claw, he drew her chair.

"Did you sleep well?"

"I did, yes," she replied, surprised he even thought to ask.

"And the castle? Is it to your liking?"

"I explored a little," she admitted. "You have a lovely piano."

"Which? There are many," he replied.

"I found it in a room overlooking the garden. It was... cream, not white, but the sharps and flats were gold instead of black. It was lovely."

"It is yours."

"Mine?"

"All things in this castle are now yours," Beast said, his rumbling voice so serious, his expression so intense, she had to believe him.

"All?" *But the fourth floor of the east wing*, she thought, betting his previous warning still held. She didn't ask.

"This is now your home, and as this is your home, we are all your servants."

"We?" Ana asked. Her brows knit, but the dragon's expression never changed. "Hora told me she and I are the only humans in the castle."

"You are, but there are many more living souls here."

"I've seen no one. Nothing but the statues."

"You should eat before your meal goes cold."

Lifting a skeptical brow at Beast, Ana raised the domed cover on the small platter to reveal a plate of her favorite foods—griddle cakes topped with summer berries and honey, fat sausages speckled with sage, and fluffy eggs scrambled to perfection. A small pot sat beside an empty teacup.

"I don't understand. How did you know my preferences? Where is the staff? Who made this?"

How had they known her dress size before she'd ever arrived at the castle? With each discovery she made, she only found more mysteries and questions awaiting answers.

"Whose room am I in? Surely this dress belongs to someone."

"It belongs to you." His gruff voice unnerved her.

No matter how she asked or pleaded, Beast told her nothing. She settled for eating, savoring a hot meal while he brooded across the long table. Hora's warning returned to her in a stroke of wisdom. Should she dare to question his kindness and risk unraveling it all? Was it so bad to be the pampered pet of a dragon instead of his abused servant?

No.

"Could you love a creature like me?" he asked suddenly.

Anastasia froze, a forkful of eggs halfway to her mouth. "There are many types of love. Love between friends, love

95   VIVIENNE SAVAGE

between a child and mother...." *Of course he means love between friends. He's a dragon. I'm a human. What was I thinking?* she chastised herself, feeling ridiculous for almost jumping to conclusions.

"But could you love me?" he asked again.

"I honestly don't know," she replied. "You frighten me sometimes, and I barely have known you more than a handful of hours. We're strangers to one another." What an absurd, terrifying question.

Beast nodded and rose from the table. "Enjoy your meal and the freedom of the castle grounds as you please."

He left the room, long tail the last to leave her sight as it dragged behind him and through the doors.

Ana slumped in her seat, stomach quivering. What sort of question had that been?

At least Beast had the goodwill to ask, however, unlike Edward who had used strength as his tool. His memory soured her mood, and with her appetite lost, she abandoned the dining room and set out to explore the castle grounds in daylight.

A narrow stone path she hadn't noticed the previous night wound around the side of the castle. It followed the barrier wall, which she kept her distance from, fearing Beast would swoop down upon her with accusations of attempted escape.

Or perhaps he wouldn't notice. Tempted to skirt closer to the wall, she studied it and her surroundings for signs of Beast lurking nearby. Above her, branches swayed with the mountain breeze, and a flower-scented wind kissed her cheeks. She searched the oversized castle windows for a hint of a draconic shadow and saw nothing.

Lack of guidance or oversight provoked the adventurer in her. She moved to the wall and rose on tiptoe, leaning on both hands to look over the ledge of the stone barrier fencing her into the castle grounds.

The view down the steep drop-off made her stomach twist and flip. *Who in their right mind built a castle on the edge of a cliff? Dragons, obviously.* Then again, the castle itself seemed ill-suited for his size despite its lofty, vaulted ceilings and immense rooms.

"Have you lost your way?"

Ana whirled around to face the dragon. In her haste, she stumbled, and her back slammed against unyielding stone. Pieces crumbled away from a hairline fissure and tumbled to the misty depths below.

"I didn't hear you." For such a large beast, he moved silently as a cat.

"You must take care," Beast said, studying her. He leaned down and close enough for Ana to watch her own reflection in his enormous eyes. "There are many old places on these castle grounds where you could be injured."

"Oh. I see. Then I shall be on my way to return to the cas—"

"I could show you them if you desire, so that you learn your way."

VIVIENNE SAVAGE

She would have been glad to return to the castle alone and tuck herself away in the corner of her room again if his expression didn't strike her as earnest and hopeful.

"Is there so much more to see than a decrepit stone wall?" she asked.

"Much more," he said. "Come. I will show you." He gestured with a claw toward the narrow path she'd taken then fell into a casual step alongside her.

Beast's close proximity warmed her like a magical furnace, and after a few yards, Ana found herself drifting closer to him and soaking it in. She'd have to adjust to the cool mountain air or search the depths of her new wardrobe for a heavy cloak.

"Are you cold?" he asked.

"A little."

"You'll find many things in the wardrobe upstairs suitable to your needs and desires. You need only look and claim whatever you fancy," he reminded her.

"I'll keep that in mind." And perpetually wonder who had worn such delightful garments before they came into her possession. A surge of pity overtook her, and she worried for the displaced, mystery residents of the castle.

Unless... could this be the famed castle of the Witch Queen?

No. It couldn't be. The castle grounds would be in shambles, razed and ruined from the war. Everything she'd seen was pristine so far.

From the left, an immense fruit orchard arose from

a stretch of land in the eastern yards of the castle grounds. White and pink apple blossoms fluttered in the cool breeze above bushes laden with white flowers. Her mouth watered at the sight of plump, ripe fruit dangling from some of the branches, and the scent of magic washed over her.

He noticed her watchful eyes. "Does it interest you?"

"It does," she admitted. "Would it upset you if I were to visit? I've never seen an enchanted garden."

Beast shook his massive head. "No. You may come and go. Many of the trees grow more than apples and will produce cherries or peaches at times."

A truly experienced magician must have created such a marvel. Her eyes lit up as she turned to him. "Thank you."

The grounds unfolded before them, revealing more to the mountaintop than an abandoned castle. Multiple structures of stone and wood dotted the grounds, from stables to an armory.

As they walked, she studied her unusual companion. He gleamed in the sunlight, each gilded scale sparkling as he moved. One of her hands hovered out to touch him, anxious to explore his glossy hide. Were his scales as smooth as they appeared? She caught herself at the last moment and laced her fingers together against her dress.

"There is a pond a short way up this path." He gestured to a trail between a dense line of hedges too narrow for his large body to traverse.

Ana lingered at the entrance but made no move to travel further, reluctant to explore deeper into the mountain

VIVIENNE SAVAGE

wilderness by herself. Instead, she gestured to a clearing across the way.

"What's that over there? Is it a graveyard?" Ana asked.

"It is nothing," the dragon rumbled, only to cross to her opposite side and obstruct her view of the tastefully decorated mourning ground.

The small cemetery made a stark contrast against the rest of the fortress, the headstones gleaming black marble rising tall, topped with beautiful figures in a perpetual dance. Ana's brows raised, and then she turned to gaze up at him. "I wouldn't call a graveyard nothing," she protested. "Are those the graves of the castle's former inhabitants?"

In an instant, he snapped, from docile afternoon companion to fanged terror. He towered above her and snarled, "I said it is nothing!"

She shrank away and backward a step. "Apologies. I should return to the castle. Th-thank you," she stammered.

Beast remained as she hurried away.

"Princess Anastasia?" Hora called to her as she entered the keep.

Ana rushed past the castle's matron with tears rushing down her cheeks. She didn't stop until she reached the safety of her room and slammed the door shut behind her. With quaking limbs, Ana leaned back against the door and dropped her face into her hands.

"What have I done?' she whispered.

Ana threw herself across the bed and sobbed herself to

sleep. Sometime later, she stirred to the sight of a blue sky beyond her window. A handsome, old-fashioned clock on the wall told her barely an hour had passed.

The nap had left her refreshed but no less wary of her surly yet hospitable host, and she regretted picking over her breakfast. Her belly rumbled to protest its empty state.

Tap tap.

Ana's gaze swung around to her left where the curtains billowed in the wind. A blue bird had flown in through the open window and landed on a small table below it. The creature tapped its beak against a covered silver platter until Ana ventured over for a look and raised the lid. Steam rose from a bowl of creamy tomato soup served with thick slices of dark bread.

"Do you want some?" She pinched a morsel of the bread and offered it to the bird.

At the conclusion of her lunch for two, she peeked into the hall. With no sign of Hora or Beast within view, she meandered into the wide corridor and made the library her only friend. The books provided her entertainment, its expansive shelves her security. She read until the sky darkened beyond the window, and without clouds, it became an infinite plane of midnight velvet speckled with glittering celestial bodies.

Dinner had long passed by the time she returned to her private bedchamber with a bucket in hand. She found her room undisturbed save for the removal of her lunch tray and

VIVIENNE SAVAGE

the scent of roses in the air. Blinking, she proceeded forward to the bathing room and found it transformed.

Several luxurious burgundy rugs covered the cool floor beneath her bare feet when she moved inside to investigate. Steam arose from the bath nearby, allowing her to pick out notes of other oils she favored. A hint of citrus from bergamot. The musky aroma of sandalwood. Like a child, she clapped her hands then hurried over to trail her fingers through the water.

The perfect temperature.

"This can't be real. This isn't the same tub; I know how this bathroom appeared this morning," she muttered.

But it was real. All real and hers. The tub was embedded in a tall stone slab, and a bather would have to walk up several stairs to step deep within its basin. She stripped out of her clothing and pinned her hair before settling into the water. Its embrace sapped her strength and invigorated her all at once, a strange contrast.

Afterward, she dressed in a silk night rail and dressing gown before returning on velvet-lined slippers to the bedroom. Those had also awaited her in the bathing room.

How peculiar. A castle ruled by a dragon with all of the modern conveniences of the recent years he could never appreciate. She doubted Beast could even dip one of his feet into the tub, and giggled at the thought of him trying.

Did dragons bathe at all? He certainly didn't smell objectionable—a little earthy, like moist soil and smoke, but not awful.

"I can make the best of this," she announced to no one in particular before crawling into the bed. Someone had turned the sheets down the way her mother once did, back when the queen still had a stable mind.

Ana nestled into the bed and fell fast asleep, for once without worries and without fears.

His hair reminded her of fire—wild but not unkempt, barely tamed waves reaching his broad shoulders. As he had before, he wore a kilt in the fashion of the people from Cairn Ocland, though she didn't recognize the tartan from her history lessons. Most of the Oclanders had perished during the Beast Wars, beaten back by the King of Dalborough, and the remaining clans had scattered to escape persecution from the west and slavery from the opportunistic Langese people of the south.

They were such proud people. *Such proud, handsome people, too,* she thought, staring into his bright hazel eyes. He appeared as uncertain as she did and hung back to study her.

"You need not fear me," he spoke up first.

"Whoever said I feared you? Maybe I only wanted to stand back for a moment to admire you from afar," she retorted, keeping her voice light and playful. Flirtatious.

His frown deepened and a wrinkle formed between his brows. His surprise made Ana doubt whether or not he was a fabrication of some dream or a magical construct of the castle

VIVIENNE SAVAGE

she'd found after wandering from her bed in the middle of the night.

Is this a waking figment of my imagination or a sleeping fantasy? She recognized each step of the garden down to the blades of untamed grass poking between the stones on the ground.

Deciding it was definitely a dream, and a very pleasant one to converse with a young man who didn't paw her, she approached him first. An indescribable urgency like she'd never felt before made her run her fingers through his hair and smooth his untamed waves back from his handsome face. He leaned into her touch.

It wasn't proper for a young man and woman to be together alone and unchaperoned. Her mother would have had a fit, and despite the man committing no wrongdoing, her father would have had him thrown into the dungeons for a day or so for having the audacity to enjoy her company, just to remind him of his place and all.

Thinking back, she realized her father was more of an ass than she'd thought.

Anastasia felt a smug sense of satisfaction in doing what she wanted in her very own dreamworld, with her very own handsome man from the so-called Savage Plains.

"You are one of the Beastmen from Ocland, aren't you?" she asked gently. In some ways, he reminded her of an animal himself. When he pressed his cheek into her fingers and closed his eyes, he resembled a dog happy to greet his master, as did the way his nostrils flared when he breathed her in before letting his nose skim over her wrist. She shivered.

"Beastmen? Yes. We were called that once."

"Then why are you here?" she asked, probing.

"Where else would I be?" he replied, grinning easily. The consternation had melted away, leaving an easygoing smile in its place. The tension shattered.

"Riding the plains to the east of this mountain on the back of one of your animals," she teased. She could easily imagine him astride a griffin, a wild one who had retained his spirit and served out of loyalty and companionship, not because it had been stolen as an egg and slowly had its will broken.

Her sleeping mind had conjured up the best kind of man, finer than her deceased betrothed and without the condescending bravado. She felt like the nameless warrior would protect her—not endanger or cause harm.

The thought made her giggle, and her laughter, of course, made the young man tilt his head down to look at her. Studying him, she didn't think he was as close to her age as she'd previously assumed. He was probably nearer to thirty, but built and chiseled like a laborer. Or a knight who had seen many battles.

Her dream mind should have conjured him naked, so she could better appreciate his muscles. Instead, he wore a white linen shirt, unfastened at the neck to reveal the dip between the muscles of his fine chest. Brazen confidence drove her to place a palm above his heart, and he froze.

VIVIENNE SAVAGE

"What courage you have to brave this fortress," he whispered. "But will you wield the same tenacity to free me from my imprisonment?"

"Are you a captive here as well?" she asked.

"All is not as it seems, lass. You'll come to see that in time."

Then the nameless man raised her hand from his chest and kissed her knuckles before touching his cheek to her palm. He hadn't shaved recently, and stubble abraded her palm, its color as red as the auburn locks on his shoulders.

Giving in to impulse, she rose up to her toes and brushed their lips together.

Anastasia had intended sweet, but what she received was searing passion in return. The young man's strong arms enfolded her and, in the next second, drew her flush to the masculine length of his torso. Her knees turned to jelly.

Then his tongue probed her lips, urging them to part. No longer concerned with the weakness in her legs, she melted against him and wrapped her arms around his shoulders. As their tongues met, she savored the wild, smoky taste of him.

Long after the kiss ended, she remained pressed to the prince of her fantasies. Their brows touched, and those beautiful, hazel-green eyes remained on her face—beautiful, hauntingly familiar eyes.

"Will you tell me your name?" she whispered.

"Perhaps another time."

"Why not now?"

Another crease lined his brow.

"Are you unable to tell me?" she asked curiously.

"No... I... I believe I can."

"Then please share your name with me. I've told you mine."

He was all hard muscle against her body, and the presence of a shirt saddened her. It had been easier to admire those chiseled lines when he was bare-chested.

At first, her companion said nothing. She glided her fingers through his bold, red strands, and after a moment, he whispered, "My name is Alistair. Prince Alistair of Clan TalDrach. A name I have not said in quite a while."

Ana awakened to a bird's song from the open window, confused and disoriented by the shift. One moment, she'd been hand in hand with a handsome figment of her imagination, and in the next, she was stirring in bed.

A dream. It had been only a dream after all.

"Of course it was a dream," she muttered. "The Cairn Ocland royal family is long gone."

While they were a secretive bunch, she thought she would have known for sure if there was a prince. All she'd ever heard about thirteen years ago was their infamous Witch Queen, a fearsome warrior enchantress who rode into battle on the back of a black dragon.

Ana bathed for a long time and donned a thick, wool dress, finding them in no short supply in the wardrobe.

VIVIENNE SAVAGE

She took her breakfast alone without the company of the beast. He never showed, much to her disappointment. Part of her had hoped to see him again and apologize for poking what was obviously a sore spot for him.

It was a graveyard. Of that, I am certain, Ana decided. Beast had lost someone close to him, and the wounds hadn't yet healed.

A morning exploration on the third level discovered an aviary filled with songbirds. Afterward, she spent lunch in the library and discovered a room adjacent to it through a small door filled from wall to wall with tomes on alchemy. Books covered every subject in the field from the poisons of Liang to the healing tonics of Creag Morden.

Absorbed in a book about elemental magic, she missed her chance to eat, or thought she had until she emerged an hour after noon to find a tray awaiting her on a small table.

Why hadn't Hora greeted her?

After enjoying hot soup and bread, she sipped tea and surrendered her afternoon to reading about the flora of Cairn Ocland. She wanted something to discuss with the man of her dreams and giggled when she realized how preposterous she sounded.

As if a dream man cared what she spoke to him about.

Regardless, she became absorbed with the pages, pages that had seen much love. She found notes in the margins written in a delicate script, but she didn't understand the language. Something told her it was a woman's handwriting.

A simple translation spell transformed the words from the Oclandian language to her native tongue.

The Witch Queen, she thought. *This must be her book.*

Ana returned the ribbon between the pages and closed the leather-bound tome, deciding to take it to her room for reading by candlelight in bed. When she emerged from the small alchemy haven, the sight of Beast passing the window startled her, and she nearly dropped her book.

Was he looking for her?

She glanced at the doors and pursed her lips. Since her arrival, she'd noticed certain areas of the castle had dragon-sized entries. The magnificent library had an enormous open space, more than large enough for him to comfortably sit. Odd, she thought, but perhaps the Witch Queen had enjoyed pleasant evenings here with her fearsome dragon on guard.

Maybe she would invite him to join her next time. The rest of her life was a long time indeed, too long to live in disharmony with her host.

Chapter 5

ANASTASIA CARRIED HER basket to the next tree, her face raised to study its bounty of sweet fruit.

The palace orchards spanned across acres, seemingly home to every fruit she could desire. She hadn't expected to find the tropical, orange-fleshed citrus fruits native to Liang's southern climates, but she'd discovered them and rejoiced.

"One would think this orchard was fairy-blessed in addition to its enchantments, the way the fruit sways so heavily from each bough but never bends the branches."

Hora chuckled. The matron offered her no assistance, and that was well and fine with Ana. She needed the exercise, unacquainted with sitting in a library all day despite her tendencies to value her studies.

"Tell me, Hora, why do you remain here alone with him?"

"Where else would I go?" the older woman asked.

"Another castle perhaps. Your meals are… incredible. I imagine any lord or wealthy noble would be thrilled to have you among the staff. Or even a husband! Is there a husband?" She knew so little about the woman who crossed her path on occasion.

"There was once, but he is long gone and passed from

this world," Hora said. "I suppose the truth is... I am happy here. My fondest and happiest memories are of serving this household. It binds me here. I can think of no better place I would be."

Ana bent to pluck up a fallen apple, its flesh pink and creamy white beneath the peel, unusual and different from the reds and greens she knew at home with their white inside. "Even with Beast?" She glanced up at her companion.

"Even with Beast. He's a good one, though he is inexperienced with young, human women. You must excuse him."

"He asked me a strange question once," Ana murmured. "If I could love him."

"He means no insult to you with his questions."

"I realized it, but in the days since he yelled at me, there are no questions at all. He hasn't come to me for company," she said, sighing, "and I don't know where to find him. One would think a creature of his immense size wouldn't succeed at hiding so well."

"Oh dear," Hora said. The woman sighed. "He is ashamed to have lost his temper and scared you."

"I'm ashamed to have fled in terror as I did," Ana admitted. "My emotions got the best of me."

"Which is natural, Princess Anastasia. We all have emotions and lose control of them at times."

Basket full, Ana stepped away from the trees and shaded her eyes against the sun's glare. "Does he always vanish like

VIVIENNE SAVAGE

this? How does a dragon even hide?"

"We all have our secrets," Hora replied. "Give him time, Princess, and he'll come out again. I promise you that. Shall we return?"

Ana sighed. "I suppose so. Part of me had hoped he would see us."

"In time, sweet girl. He knows he's made a blunder, and he'll come to you once he can conquer his pride."

"All right." Ana forced a quiet smile and buffed one of the apples against her dress. "I plan to leave these in the dining room as a peace offering. If you cross paths, will you let him know?"

"Of course. He's fond of these apples."

While quiet and resistant to sharing information about Beast, Hora was a font of information. Ana studied the old woman. "You served the royal family, Hora. What were they like?"

"Kind," she replied. "They were kind."

"The queen?"

"Exceptional. She treated all members of this castle staff as if we were family. We wanted for nothing. To her, we weren't merely servants, we were cherished and loved." She sighed.

"And her dragon?"

"Rua was as protective as any dragon could be of his rider. He gave his life to protect her, and she carried on the fight for some time afterward to protect this castle."

"And then she fell," Ana whispered.

"Yes. They were outnumbered and taken by surprise."

"But why? I've read about the war and an account from King Frederick during history lessons. My tutors say Cairn Ocland brought it on themselves for denying the Creator and practicing... awful things." She swallowed as heat surged to her cheeks. The Oclanders were seen as uncivilized and hedonistic.

"Greed. It had nothing to do with our customs or our failure to worship your god. It was greed. These mountains are filled with treasure, and it isn't all gold, Princess Anastasia. Your father knows of the flowers that grow here, but I believe I know what truly lured him to attack."

"You do?" Ana's eyes widened with interest.

"There is a legend in Liang. A man who drinks the blood from a dragon's heart is a man who may live forever. But it is not so easy to claim such a prize. Dragons incinerate upon death. They burn and nothing remains but ash, so a hunter must be swift or his treasure is lost forever."

Horror overwhelmed Ana and turned her belly into a cold, hard lump of sickness. It rose to her throat. "That's abhorrent, Hora! How would someone know such a thing is true?"

"No one knows. I don't believe anyone has ever succeeded, yet many believe myth and risk their lives to try."

"No, my father would never do something so horrible."

"Yet he has sent slayers, more than one, after Beast for a mere flower. One very nearly succeeded. The assassin I

VIVIENNE SAVAGE

mentioned to you came the closest of all the mercenaries who darkened these grounds."

Emotion clenched Ana's heart with the unyielding power of an iron fist. "I never agreed with his vendetta against Beast," she whispered, "but he did it with good intentions."

"Have good intentions ever legitimized murder?"

Mute with shame, Ana shook her head.

She returned indoors with Hora, left her peace offering to Beast while claiming a small portion of the fruit to stock the ceramic bowl in her bedroom, and spent an hour up to her neck in a steaming bubble bath while she read a romance novel from the queen's collection.

Wrinkled and relaxed, she tucked herself into bed with the same book, only for exhaustion to pull her under before the story concluded.

Anastasia had begun to look forward to her dreams of Prince Alistair. He never disappointed her and had become company in her otherwise quiet, lonely existence. Fleeting moments with Hora didn't satisfy her need for human companionship, but her dreams with Alistair did.

The other side of her dreams delivered her to a place where sounds of activity and merriment filled the castle grounds with evidence of abundant life. There was a vibrancy and energy present that her waking world lacked. Birds trilled from the trees, butterflies and fat bumblebees flit between flowers, and laughter drifted to her on the flower-scented breeze.

As before, the smiling faces greeted her, but she did little more than smile and wave in return, moving on swift feet toward the back gardens where she always found her prince. He waited for her by a towering line of hedges.

"You came," he said, taking her hands.

"Did you doubt I would?" What an odd thing to say, she thought, giggling at the ridiculousness of it all.

Arm in arm, they walked through the gardens and spoke of inconsequential things. Over the course of her many dreams, she'd discovered they shared multiple hobbies from favorite books to horse riding. Of course, such was to be expected of any prince she dreamed up. Why conjure someone boring or repulsive?

"Would you like to see a secret place, my beautiful princess?"

"What is left that we have not seen?"

His smile broadened as he gestured to a rose-covered arch, the entrance to the castle's hedge maze. Ana had passed it by several times during her waking explorations. The hedges were overgrown and imposing. The maze was one of the few places that seemed unkempt and wild, allowed to grow free and untamed by man.

"Do you know the way to the center?" she asked.

"I do," he told her. "But what shall I receive if I lead you there?"

Ana nibbled her bottom lip. She suspected he was fishing for another kiss, but if it was a dream, what did it matter what she said to him? Stalling, she pressed a palm to his chest

VIVIENNE SAVAGE

and felt the strong rhythm pounding beneath her touch. She stroked downward and caressed him, thrilled when he voiced no complaints.

"Well?" he pressed.

"If you lead me to the center of the maze... you shall receive... *me*. All of me."

Chapter 6

Kᴵɴɢ Mᴏʀɢᴀɴ sᴛᴇᴘᴘᴇᴅ from the carriage and onto Dalborovian soil for the first time since he and his wife abandoned Ana at Darkmoor Castle. Lorelei had been ill and more disagreeable than usual, and he'd been forced to spirit her away in the middle of the night. Now he regretted it. Perhaps if he'd waited out her shrieking spell, if he'd been in the castle, Anastasia wouldn't have snapped.

Was she falling prey to her mother's mania after all? Had she inherited the ugly sickness?

He could think of no other reason why she would perform an act of violence against their allies. The incident made their procurement of the twilight rose all the more vital, if both his daughter and his wife were destined to suffer from the fairy dementia.

A daunting sight loomed before him, a castle beyond cold iron gates that wouldn't open to permit him inside. He lacked the manpower and the experience to take on the dragon of Benthwaite, and with no alternative to save his daughter, he turned to the only people who could.

Could he make them see reason and understand that Anastasia hadn't been herself? He wanted to see Edward with his own two eyes and speak with the boy to find out what happened. But first, he had to get on the castle grounds.

Two impassive guards stared at him.

"I've come to speak with King Frederick. Did my message not arrive? I expected a royal welcome."

"We are aware," one guard stated in a cool voice. "But your royal welcome has long worn thin."

"Please. I only wish to speak to them of peace and make amends for whatever has taken place," Morgan said.

"You must wait for King Frederick's emissary," the second guard said. "Only he can determine whether or not our monarch finds you worthy enough to enter."

It wasn't in the proud king's nature to be obedient, but with Anastasia's safety at stake, he would do anything. He would walk on coals burned by the fires of the dragon's breath if it meant his daughter would be returned safe from harm.

Morgan would even grovel to the king of another nation.

For her safety, he thought, making the words his mantra during the humiliating hour he was left to wait outside of Darkmoor. At last, a messenger arrived in the wealthy finery of King Frederick's most loyal servants, a leather surcoat embroidered with the familial crest, a jagged dagger over a slaughtered unicorn.

"You have much courage to come here, King Morgan," the royal emissary said to him. "His Royal Highness has decided to allow you to enter his audience chamber. I am to accompany you."

"Very well."

King Morgan's guards moved to follow, but the emissary held up a hand. "You and only you. They must remain here."

The elite soldiers of his personal guard regiment stiffened and bristled. Hands hovered over swords.

"We accompany King Morgan at all times," one of the gruff men said, "and will not be parted from his side on foreign lands."

"Your Majesty," Williford murmured, "I do not like the sound of this, allowing you to enter a potentially dangerous situation."

Morgan nodded curtly. "Neither do I, but we are mere guests in another land. My daughter's life is at stake, Williford. For as long as the princess is in danger, we must each do our part to rescue her."

Six uncertain glances were exchanged among the royal guardsmen, but Williford sighed and relented first. "As you wish, sire. We will await you here." They stepped back and fell into formation as the messenger led Morgan up the long road to the castle doors.

Darkmoor Castle earned its name by being constructed from a black stone mined from a nearby mountain range. Windows fashioned from volcanic glass muted the light, shading the interior of the castle as an act of necessity. King Frederick's skin was sun sensitive.

Their footsteps echoed through the bleak and empty halls, every inch of the corridors dominated by shadows.

Black curtains bordered the darkened windows, used to rob the rooms of any light that wasn't generated by candles.

Such a cold and dreary place, he thought. *How could I ever have condemned my bright and vibrant Ana to such a place?*

As they approached the audience chamber, his heart slammed in his chest. How badly could she have possibly wounded the boy? She was only a girl, after all, and not particularly strong. While he had indulged her desire to practice archery, he had drawn the line at blades. Ana knew nothing of fighting or knifeplay beyond what she observed among the men during training or competitions.

Two men flanking the grand doors to the audience chamber pushed them inward, revealing the candlelit room of the king's receiving room. Three high-back, onyx thrones sat at the edge of a high dais, its tall design intended to make the visitor feel tiny and insignificant.

It worked.

Frederick's scarred and misshapen face glared down at him from the middle stone. None of the three spoke a greeting, and in a matter of seconds, Morgan lost his carefully rehearsed speech.

"I thank you for accepting my visit," he said to the three royals.

Queen Brunhilda's baleful gaze cut through Morgan then slid to the side. "What right does he have to be here when his little whore nearly killed our boy?" she demanded.

"Silence, Brunhilda. How unkingly would I be to send

away our neighbor who comes in desperation once more to us?"

Edward sat in his throne to the right of his father, bulky and large bandages visible beneath his clothes. Sweat glistened against his pale brow, the aftermath of a horrible fever according to the information gleaned by Morgan's spymaster. After several touch-and-go days, he was fortunate to be alive.

The king forced a smile. "My son still lives. For a time, we were not certain if he would survive the injuries your ingrate inflicted, but the healer has assured us he shall recover. The fever is almost past now, and though he should be abed, he insisted he should join us here to greet you."

"Frederick, I apologize. I truly am sorry for whatever happened between them. I only know it isn't in Anastasia's nature to harm anyone. *Anyone*," he repeated.

"You are wrong," Edward said in a hitched breath. A servant hurried forward to assist the young man when he showed an inclination to straighten in the seat.

"Please, I would like to know what happened, to hear it in your words," Morgan said.

"She attacked me without provocation," Edward said. "Perhaps I was wrong to visit her bedchamber without a chaperone, but as it was the night before our wedding, I asked only for a kiss." He groaned and slouched in the seat, tilting his head back. A maid dabbed his forehead with a cloth.

King Frederick and Queen Brunhilda listened quietly, but the latter shook with rage. Moving like a nervous bird,

VIVIENNE SAVAGE

she hurried from her seat and tore the cloth from the servant's hand to dote over her son instead.

"He should return to his rest," the queen said to her husband.

"No, Mother. I will stay."

While Anastasia had been unhappy with his decision to wed her to their family, nothing about her personality or even her behavior leading up to their travel had indicated she would try to take his life.

It didn't make sense. Nothing about it added up.

"What happened next?" Morgan asked. "Certainly a girl couldn't overpower you. You're a strong, strapping lad."

"She gave the kiss, and then she assaulted me with one of her hair ornaments before I realized what was happening."

Morgan flinched. "Perhaps she was frightened—"

"Only a kiss," Edward said again with difficulty. "It is only by great fortune I continue to live… a maid happened by her room and saw the door ajar."

"Now why are you here?" Brunhilda demanded. "Certainly you've not come for aid."

Morgan raised his chin. "I do. Perhaps I have no right to ask it, but the dragon has taken my daughter."

"Then the beast is in good company," Brunhilda retorted as she returned to her seat.

Frederick chuckled and patted her knee. "Never let it be said I am not a kind and benevolent man. I understand you fear for your daughter's well-being, but you must understand my predicament, Morgan. She attempted to take the life of my only son the night before they were to be wed."

"I don't know what she was thinking, but I can hardly believe Anastasia would do such a thing."

"And yet she did," the King of Dalborough said imperiously. "And if you doubt the veracity of my son's account so greatly, you may retrieve your spoiled princess by your own power."

"No! Please. I believe my wife's affliction may have affected Anastasia as well," Morgan said with a heavy heart. "I ask—no, I beseech you to take pity upon me and understand she may have been wild with insanity. My daughter means the world to me, and I would do anything to protect her."

"Then you must pay the blood price," Frederick said, "and we will absolve her of the crime."

"Of course." He swallowed back his apprehension, not daring to imagine what price they would demand. He'd empty his coffers if it meant getting Ana back. "I want your word Anastasia will remain unharmed and unspoiled, returned promptly to my kingdom without punishment."

"No," Edward said. "I still want her."

Morgan blanched, and Frederick raised a brow. "Even after she nearly took your life, son?"

The prince's strained smile unnerved Morgan. "Yes, Father. It may take some time for me to recover from my injuries. When the time comes, I will hunt and slay this beast. But she is to return here with me. That is my price."

"And if I choose to say no?" Morgan asked. A cold sweat cooled his skin.

"You take your chances with the dragon. Perhaps he will not eat her. Perhaps I'll gain my strength, we'll raid the castle, and we'll claim her anyway but as a prisoner."

Morgan felt sick to his stomach. This wasn't how he imagined the outcome. He'd thought he could bribe them heavily with money and promises of attaining great treasure from the dragon's hoard. Had he known Edward's heart, he would have attempted to mount his own rescue efforts and save her with his smaller army.

"Very well," Morgan whispered. "I agree to your terms. Help me get her back."

"Then let us plan," Frederick said with a quiet chuckle, "and determine what goods we desire from Creag Morden as the blood price for your daughter's treachery."

Chapter 7

FAILURE. AGAIN. NOTHING had gone according to Alistair's plan.

The fairy was right. He had the temperament of a spoiled child, and if he ever wanted to become a man of two legs and two arms again, he'd have to learn to control it.

He hunted by evening and slept on the castle's fourth floor by night, aware of her exploring the library below him. He looked in once at her and was almost certain she saw him. But she said nothing.

Today was a new chance, however, and a fresh morning. He chose not to pursue her, but neither did he hide, instead spending his time in the garden beyond the ballroom where he lazily watched the clouds and wondered what it would be like to sit in a chair again. To lie in a bed. To hold a woman in his arms. Something he'd only done twice in his human life before that ability was stolen from him. Sighing, he closed his eyes and imagined.

Alistair smelled Ana long before she walked into sight. Roses and night-blooming jasmine. The aroma of roasted meat and ripe cheese wafting from the oversized basket in her arms couldn't mask Ana's scent.

Raising his head, he watched her through drowsy eyes.

"Oh." The princess came to an abrupt stop near the blackberry hedge. Fretful eyes gazed across the distance, and she backpedaled. "Forgive me, Beast. I didn't mean to disturb your rest."

"You haven't disturbed me." He lurched to his feet and bowed his head to avoid towering above her, but the sun cast his shadow over Ana's tiny body. "Did you wish to use the garden?"

"Hora packed a picnic. I thought I'd enjoy it here."

Wrong. Hora had nothing to do with its packing. They had no deliveryman and no workers and staff to milk livestock and fetch eggs from the hens. The castle did it. The damned castle created everything, both a gift and his curse, providing anything he needed and, by proxy, anything Ana desired.

He glanced at the book also tucked under her arm. "You came to read."

"I came to enjoy my afternoon. I can read about wind magic another time," she assured him. "Now would you like to share this meal or not??"

"Aye, lass, that would be grand," he stated firmly.

Ana closed the distance between them and set everything into its proper place. She shook out a blanket from the basket and spread it across the thick grass, then took a seat and situated her skirts. The indigo color, dark as the ocean at twilight, suited her fair skin and red hair.

But Ana could probably wear a bath towel and look no

less fetching. He sighed, and the noise was so loud, it startled her. She jumped and gazed up at him with large eyes.

"Apologies," he said.

"It's all right," she murmured, returning to her task. "I'm not sure there's much in here to fill your belly, but I suppose we'll see, yes?"

The enchanted basket yielded a veritable bounty of goods, their quantity too large to fit within a normal container. She removed a whole ham, thick slices of roast beef, one loaf of herb-studded bread, cheese, fruits, onion jam, and other light delicacies. A bottle of honey mead rounded out the meal, and Alistair promptly coveted her small hands and ability to partake of the fine vintage.

"Should I pour you some?" she asked him in a polite tone.

Skeptical, he raised the ridge above his left eye, doubting it would be enough to do more than wet his mouth. A splash on his tongue. He missed mead. Of all the mortal conveniences he no longer enjoyed, drinking ranked at the top. Though there had been a desperate time some years ago when he'd raided a village to the deep south, tore the roof from a tavern, and plucked two kegs from behind the bar.

"Your company is more fulfilling than any meal or drink. I…." He hesitated and snorted smoke, disused to taking responsibility for his actions. Hadn't the blasted fairy told him to learn humility? "I apologize for my behavior. Frightening you wasn't my intention."

Surprise flitted across her features. "I didn't mean to pry,

  VIVIENNE SAVAGE

Beast, so I owe you an apology as well." After serving a small portion for herself, she raised the ceramic platter bearing the ham and set it on the blanket within his reach. "Go on. Enjoy the ham. It's delicious, and I have more than enough."

The food beckoned him with its spiced, honey-glazed slices. His nostrils flared, but then he tucked his head low and glanced away while his stomach rumbled with anticipation.

"Would Hora appreciate help in the kitchen? I feel awful that she runs everything alone."

"Would you know what to do in a kitchen?" He licked the sharp edge of a tooth.

"I'm not entirely helpless. and I suppose I could learn. What else am I to do all day?"

"Your studies, perhaps." He eyed the ham again, and when her eyes were away, focused on a distant butterfly circling in the breeze, he gobbled the delicious morsel in a bite.

"My studies?" Her eyes slowly raised to him from the beautiful insect. "Do you have a tutor from the Academy here hidden away?"

Alistair cursed himself. He wasn't supposed to know that she had been days from leaving the palace behind for a life of academia and magic. He stared at her in alarm, his mouth full of unchewed ham. "Hrm," he said, unable to speak. He tried to chew discretely.

She glanced at the empty plate then his mouth. Was that a smile on her face?

Alistair shook his head and spoke once he swallowed.

"There are no tutors here, only you and I," he said, "but I thought the best magicians among your kind were self-taught. Will books and a laboratory to perfect your craft be sufficient, or will you need more, lass?"

"Self-taught?" She blinked again but then dropped her gaze to consider the idea. "I always have learned better from books that from teachers, though…. And I've certainly enjoyed your library since arriving, but I also don't want to make a mess of things and destroy your home. Is there a safe place for me to practice where I wouldn't catch things on fire by accident?"

Her green eyes shone with interest, and he celebrated the small victory. "I breathe fire and live in a castle of stone," he reminded her.

"Yes, but you aren't breathing fire inside, right?" She aimed a small smile up at him then dug around again in the basket. "Do you like cheese? There's a whole wheel in here I didn't notice before."

She raised the offering to him. Again, he hesitated, until she rose to her feet with it in hand. "Please. I can't enjoy my lunch alone while you go hungry. Or have you eaten?" A sly tone filled her voice, and mirth shone in her eyes.

"I have not."

"Except the ham," she added, chuckling a throaty laugh. She nudged the tip of his snout with the cheese wheel. "Please?"

Barely opening his mouth, Alistair accepted the bite-sized snack from her hands. She didn't shy away from his teeth, giving him hope that he was no longer a monster to her.

"I've never seen you eat before, but of course, there must be all sorts of wild game in the mountains for you to catch. Deer especially. My father—" She cleared her throat and continued in a subdued tone. "My father brought home a large buck once. He took my brothers with him, but I had to stay home. Hunting is not proper for a young lady."

"Why is it not proper?"

"I honestly have no idea. A princess is supposed to always look her best. She is to be polite, well-read, musical, and charming. She isn't to go traipsing about in the woods with a weapon she cannot handle. Never mind the fact that I am a better shot than half my brothers."

"A better shot with what? A bow?"

"Yes. It was the one indulgence my father allowed me when it came to weaponry, but only at targets in the garden."

"And all because you are female?"

"Yes."

"Then your human kingdoms are foolish," he growled. "Where I come from, the princesses defend their homelands with as much zeal as their male counterparts."

As far as Alistair was concerned, the supposed civilized people of the west had their priorities wrong. They raised meek girls, but he saw something more, something greater in Ana than a trophy piece.

"Dragons have princesses?" She perked up, giving him her full attention.

Alistair grumbled, and curls of smoke escaped his nostrils. She'd caught him in another mistake, the clever minx, and it only made him desire her even more. "We have many things," he said with a mysterious air, providing no clarification.

"Are families among those many things? I didn't think dragons lived in family groups at all. I've only ever heard of lone dragons living in their hoards."

"What did you believe we do?" he asked. "Father young and abandon our mates and cubs to the wilderness? Does it surprise you a dragon should have a family when we have castles?" He raised a claw to the vast estate.

"Well, to be honest, I had sort of wondered about that. The castle, I mean. You're far too large for most of the rooms. I figured you must have settled here after the Ocland royal family was driven out...."

"I have lived here alone since the King of Dalborough murdered them," he confided, neither lying nor revealing the absolute truth of his origins. He couldn't, even if he wanted, share his true identity. The fairy's curse wouldn't allow it, and he'd die if he tried.

He was dying anyway. Soon. It was only a matter of time. He'd never make her love him before the thirteenth anniversary of his changing.

Her fragile smile faded. "I'm sorry," she whispered, "that they killed everyone. They call the Oclanders barbarians, but the castle is beautiful. More lovely than Darkmoor Castle. I imagine it was full of life and laughter, love and light. It feels sad now. Lonely, but no less magnificent."

"The Oclanders were fond of festivals, and they would dance long into the night around grand bonfires with wine and song. Once a year, the king and queen would host a grand ceremony to honor their gods, and commoners from across the kingdom would travel days by horseback and on foot. They turned away no one. All were welcome to the feast. Now their numbers are too few for celebrations."

"It sounds fun. Welcoming. I imagine it was a sight to behold."

"It was…." He looked away, grateful his reptilian features hid his sorrow. "The book you brought. What's in it? Will you tell me about it?"

Her eyes lit up, and she accepted his change of topic with grace, offering no more apologies. "Wind spells. Did you know you can summon the breezes by whistling to them?"

"I have heard such calls, yes, but I have no talent for them." He paused, then added, "Nor can I whistle."

Ana's amused giggle sounded like music to his ears.

"I never knew so much could be done through weather spells. There are accounts of wizards summoning fearsome gales and bringing lightning down upon their enemies."

"Do you aspire to be such a sorceress?"

"Oh… no. I'll never be as talented as the wizards in the stories."

"How do you know?"

"I'm not good with high-level spells and still need a

wand."

His brows furrowed. "You do not have your wand?"

Ana shook her head. "It was in my bag along with the rest of my possessions."

"Then we must remedy this," Alistair concluded. "Or you must learn to cast magic with no wand at all. Mastery does not come without practice, Princess."

"You sound like my mother," she muttered.

He ignored it. "Can you summon a breeze? I imagine it would be pleasant on a sunny day."

"I can certainly try." She pulled over her book and flipped through the pages until she found what she was looking for. "To call a wind, whistle thrice in ascending tones," she read. "To send it away, whistle thrice in descending pitch. That sounds simple enough."

Alistair settled again on his belly to observe. "That it does. Give it a try then, lass."

He found it amusing to watch the way her face scrunched up in concentration. Endearing, even. Ana turned her face toward the sky and whistled as the tome instructed.

Nothing happened.

"Try again," he encouraged. "Focus on what you want. Feel the breeze through your hair and bid it to follow your whim."

This time, Ana appeared more relaxed. She closed her eyes and tilted her face toward the puffy clouds, her expression serene. Beautiful. Alistair watched her pink lips part as she drew in a breath, then purse together to whistle.

A subtle energy surrounded her. Her magical aura tickled against his scales, popping like effervescent bubbles as the cool breeze stirred the flowers and ruffled Ana's copper waves. Alistair turned his face into the welcome current of air.

"Well done."

Fallen leaves and flower petals raised into the air, lifted by the circling current and forming a ring of color around her.

"You are not so bad as you claim, Princess." His chest expanded with a rising sense of pride for the young woman who had gone unappreciated by her own people. The Oclanders would have loved her. Even the Witch Queen would have been taken with her upon the first meeting.

Ana's eyes filled with wonder. "I... I've never managed to cast magic without a wand before."

"Come, I have someplace I'd like to show you."

A deep furrow appeared on her brow before she released her spell. The petals and flowers drifted gracefully to the ground. He led her toward the northwestern cliffside overlooking the world below, and there a circle of cairn stones arose from the earth like jagged bones. Colorful veins ran throughout each one and sparkled beneath the sun.

"Many enchantresses of Ocland have meditated here in peace," he told her. "It is a place of strong magic with a connection to the rest of the world, a place for you to study and develop your talents."

Anastasia stepped ahead. He watched her eyes grow large

with excitement and the joy transform her face. She cried out with glee and whirled to face him. "It's lovely, Beast! Lovely! Truly. Thank you." The smile she bestowed was radiant, brief and fleeting as the sun peeking out from behind heavy clouds, but beautiful nonetheless. She circled the cairn first, fingers touching lightly to each stone in turn before she took a slow step inside.

He stared at her, struck dumb by her smile. Whatever words that came to mind originally faded, and he lowered his haunches to watch her step within the circle. It accepted her without question, and the area buzzed with pure magic and the mystical hum of a thousand spellcasters before her, their voice mere echoes on the breeze. "This is where the Witch Queen of Ocland made her last stand against the invaders."

A gray blanket stretched across the sky, and it only drew closer with Ana in the cairn circle. Alistair watched the progressive darkness kiss the edge of once-white clouds and bring the damp promise of rain on the wind.

"What was she like?" Ana asked, drawing his attention away from the sky.

"A discussion for another time, Princess."

"You promise to tell me?"

"I promise, but you should return indoors. A storm will be here soon, and it won't be a pleasant one."

"Will you be at dinner tonight?"

"Would you like me to be?"

"I would appreciate the company, if you're comfortable

with it. The dining hall is so large for only one person. Lonely."
Her fingers drifted over his snout, and he lived for every
second of contact.

"Yes," he said. "I have behaved like a poor host, haven't I?
I thought…." I *thought she loathed me and held me in disdain.*
It would be his pleasure to join her again. He smiled. "I will be
there."

She lowered her hands to her sides. "May I come here
whenever I please?"

Alistair mourned the loss of her touch and almost
followed her hands by instinct. "Yes," he agreed, no less sad.
He rose and moved to the side of her. "You are welcome to visit
any part of this mountain with or without me."

"Thank you, Be—" She paused and cocked her head.
"Won't you tell me your real name? It feels rude, calling you
Beast, when you're anything but."

No one but Hora had uttered his name in over a decade.
He longed for the sound of it from her lips, but he frowned
instead. The fairy had made her promise clear; he'd die if he
spoke the truth to anyone. "Perhaps my recent deeds have
earned the name," he spoke instead.

The first rumble of thunder echoed across the cliffs
and mountains peaks. He didn't move from the spot he had
claimed on the grassy mountain shelf, craving the cleansing
rain against his scales.

"Then it seems there are more secrets beyond these stones
for me to unravel. I will see you at dinner."

Beauty & the Beast

After dipping into a curtsy, she hurried back to the castle and reached the doors seconds before the sky split open and loosed a roaring downpour.

Chapter 8

MANY MORE DINNERS and meals passed between them, and as usual, Alistair asked her the same question. Ana's eyes no longer grew wide with fear, but she smiled back at him and answered in a soft voice, "I don't know. Perhaps as a friend. I do feel fond of you."

"But not love," he said.

"No, Beast. Not love."

It was one step closer than before. And with only three months left until the thirteenth anniversary, he began to wonder if death was inevitable, or if the fairy's promise was true.

Ana was the girl from his dreams, of that he had no doubt from the moment he first saw her. And while the dreams had continued since her arrival, he took comfort in them. In the daylight, he enjoyed the company of the real girl, and at night, she comforted him during what had once been fitful sleep. There had been no nightmares since he brought her to the castle.

She gave him hope that he would live.

With their misunderstandings in the past, he looked forward to meeting her at each meal. When he lost his temper, she didn't shrink back and flee. She raised her chin and stared at him in defiance, daring him to raise his voice again.

His red-haired spitfire.

"I have something to show you," he said one day, interrupting her practice in the cairn circle.

Ana glanced over a shoulder at him. Both of her hands were raised high over her head, and she was toying with the weather, occasionally bringing down a bolt of lightning into the empty fields below the mountain. She charged the air with electricity, the bite of it a strong scent in the wind. "Really?"

"Aye, something I believe you will enjoy greatly."

"As greatly as this circle? You spoil me, Sir Dragon," she teased. "You were right, by the way. I've learned more in this castle as a student at my own pace than I have with any tutors. The Witch Queen took detailed notes."

"Do you understand the language?"

"More and more. I haven't had to use the translation spells as much recently. That in itself is a difficult charm, but… I'm learning on my own now. It's very similar to our language in Creag Morden."

Alistair smiled. The Anastasia of his dreams had been as eager to learn the Oclander language as he'd been to teach it. But it was only a dream, and he'd been too shy to teach her in the real world.

"Now what must I do to receive this new surprise from you?"

"Light the sky again, Princess, and then I'll reveal it."

The skies above the castle itself were surprisingly clear, but she'd found a distant system of dense clouds on the southern horizon perfect for training purposes.

"As you wish."

Anastasia closed her eyes. A single lightning bolt was child's play, that much he remembered from his mother. He had no true propensity for magic himself, understanding only the most rudimentary spells, but he could still appreciate the difficulty and her long hours in practice.

Concentration wrinkled her brow.

"Push yourself," he encouraged.

He'd watched her practice daily in the cairn for weeks, but he knew she was capable of more. Lacking a teacher, he served as her faithful coach instead.

"I'm trying."

"To hell with trying, lass. Do it."

The clouds exploded, almost blinding Alistair. Sizzling streaks of light fell from the sky, plunging into the forest below. A tree ignited and flames billowed on the wind.

Anastasia collapsed, but Alistair was there to catch her in his huge claws. Despite her daily sessions, large and complex spells still sent her into a swoon. He held her upright until she squirmed and searched with her feet to find the ground.

"I did it. Beast, I did it!"

"That you did, Princess. I am proud of you, and you are all the more deserving of my gift. Collect yourself, and we will go."

"Thank you. I'm ready now."

He gestured for her to pass ahead of him, and they traveled together across the grounds.

"Beast, why are there no portraits of the royal family in the castle?"

"Why do you ask? And how did you come up with such a question when we are outdoors?"

"Oh, I don't know," she replied. "I thought of it much earlier, but it didn't come to me again until now. Everywhere I went at home, there seemed to be paintings of my family. But there are none here. Is it an Oclander custom?"

"Yes," Alistair replied. "Oclanders do not sit for portraits frequently, and when they do, they decorate only the familial residence."

"The fourth floor," she guessed.

"Aye."

Ana let the subject drop, but he caught her studying him as their path traveled from the courtyard and took a curve around the castle.

"Does my size no longer frighten you?" he asked.

"Not so much anymore, I don't think. When I was a girl, it took me some time to get used to the horses; they were so big compared to me, but they aren't to blame for that and neither are you. You are what you are." She pressed her lips together and clasped her hands.

She compared him to a horse. Of course, horses were gentle, lovely creatures, and he discovered a compliment

VIVIENNE SAVAGE

buried in her analogy. "Indeed. I am who I am," he agreed, only to walk alongside her in silence while controlling his misplaced anger.

It wasn't her fault.

"Were you one of the royal family's mounts?" she asked in a tentative voice. "Did you have a rider?"

His stride slowed, and then he tilted his head and gazed at her. "I've never had a rider, but I had hoped to change that this eve. Would you like to try?"

"Me? Ride you?" She swallowed. "I'm not sure I wish to dangle from your hands again. It was… disconcerting."

She called them hands, and she would never know how much joy such a simple statement had brought him. He looked down at his claws. Each individual talon hooked inward with a sharp curve, designed for spearing and mauling prey.

"I scared you that day," he stated before lowering his body against the grass and resting on his stomach. "But I will never pick you up again, my princess, unless you desire it."

"You were quite angry, not that I can blame you." She frowned down at her hands. "Beast, something has troubled me for a long while."

"Then speak your mind, and perhaps I may answer."

"Why did you attack the first adventurers who came here? I know there are always two sides to every story, and we never heard yours. Father said he sent peaceful explorers. They were to find a flower and bring it home."

While lying on his stomach with his chin against the tops

of his claws, they were eye to eye and he no longer towered above her. "This is my home," he answered. "I may be alone here, but every inch of this mountain is my home. I awakened to find humans trespassing in a place sacred to me. Stealing. Tell me, if you were to find strangers unknown to you in your personal library, taking your favorite books, would you forgive easily?"

"I'd be upset, I suppose, but... I wouldn't eat them."

"I have eaten no one," he grumbled. "I chased them from the mountain and told them their foolishness would cost their lives. I sent the king a warning." And he'd had no intention of raiding the villages or her kingdom until the king pursued him with dragonslayers and knights. The fury had overtaken him the second time, and he'd shook with intense rage while dismembering each subsequent explorer, especially the knight Sir Henry of Kirkwall, a monster from Dalborough who had killed so many of his countrymen. It had been insult to injury.

"I'm sorry my father sent men to hunt you. You see, we need that flower for my mother."

"Your mother?"

"Yes, my mother. She was a great sorceress once, but they say mortals cannot handle the strength of fairy blood for long. Over the last few years, her mind has... addled. She's a shadow of her former self," she told him, voice sad. "Stories say the twilight rose can cure her, and that it can only be found here, in these gardens. Though I guess it really is just that, a story. I've seen no magical blossoms."

"A sorceress," he repeated. His mother had been the best in Ocland. Their queen and a grand enchantress who fell for her general and mount. Within a year of their wedding, Alistair became the first dragon shifter crown prince. "Why did the king not ask for it?"

"I… I don't know. I suppose he didn't know anything intelligent lived here."

"Oh. I am but a beast after all," he agreed in a quiet voice. All the more reason to believe he was doomed to spend the remainder of his short life in a large, cumbersome dragon body, never knowing the warmth of a woman again, the comfort of a bed, the delight of a fine meal at a table again.

"Oh, no, I didn't mean it like that." Her fingers twitched, and she reached out, only to hesitate and drop her hand. "I've touched you before but never asked permission, and it was rude of me to assume. *Is* it all right that I touch you? Your scales, they're so lovely. They look like fire caught in glass. They're so warm and smooth, I can't help myself."

"If it pleases you, my princess."

Anastasia touched both hands against his warm snout. "I only meant, when he first sent explorers up here, he had no idea anyone lived in the castle. It's been thought long abandoned. Then all they knew was a dragon had taken offense. You're the first dragon I've ever met, Beast. I had no idea your kind were so intelligent and thoughtful."

Her touch filled him with turmoil and grief. How he would have loved for her to touch him as a man, but instead, she saw him as an animal. Intelligent, but an animal nonetheless. Relishing the tender contact, his eyes closed and he made a small, rumbling noise of appreciation in his chest. "Will the same happen to you one day, Anastasia? Your mind?"

"I don't know," she whispered. "Maybe, but I'm not as strong as my mother was in magic. Nothing like she'd want me to be, I'm sure."

"What do you want to be?"

"It doesn't m—" She stopped, but his mind filled in the blanks. After a last sweep of her fingers across his scales, she dropped her hands and cleared her throat.

"You wish to be powerful," he guessed.

"My desire for the power to protect myself and others is second only to my hope to one day restore my mother," Anastasia admitted. Her eyes raised to his. "Does this flower exist, Beast?"

The roses only bloomed in twilight, during an hour when Anastasia never visited the rear of the garden. He tucked his chin and sighed. "It does."

"Would you show it to me one day?"

"Yes."

Her palm returned to his cheek, and solemn, blue eyes gazed at him. "I've changed the mood of our meeting, haven't I? Why are we here?"

"I hope to give you something few humans have ever received." Her brows raised as he bowed his head low and settled on his belly. "Fly with me. This evening, you are the

Witch Queen of the mountain."

"I… but I'll fall," she protested.

"I would never let you fall. Do you trust me?"

At first, the princess watched him through wide eyes, only for a look of determination to overtake the terror. "Yes," she said. "I do."

Using the upraised scales protruding from his muscular arms and broad shoulders to boost herself onto the base of his neck, Ana squealed and grasped ahold of the pale gold horns studding his nape.

"It's almost like riding a horse!" He glanced behind him, and she quickly added. "A much larger, fire-breathing horse. Where do I hold you?"

"Where you are holding me now will do, lass. Squeeze with your legs."

"Squeeze with my legs," she repeated.

Her body emanated heat, a reminder of where they made contact. The women of Cairn Ocland wore nothing beneath their dresses, but Ana had donned something thin and made from cotton. What he wouldn't do to touch her there as a human without a barrier between them, breathing in her feminine scent before he savored the taste of her.

Anastasia released him abruptly. "Did I hurt you?"

"No. Why?"

"You groaned as if you were uncomfortable."

Very uncomfortable. Being a dragon didn't deter very male and masculine thoughts about what he wanted to do to her. Shifting his stance, Alistair adjusted the position of his wings and glanced back at her again. "Are you ready?"

"Promise you won't allow me to plummet to my death."

"I would never."

"Then I'm ready."

With a running start, he loped across the empty green space to allow her time to adjust to their motion on stable ground. Her hands were on his horns again, and her thighs squeezed snuggly with the practiced grip of a seasoned rider. His wings thrust out and swept down, lifting them into the air on one powerful flap.

Anastasia squealed and tightened her hold. Taking their first flight slow, he found a gentle current and made a lazy circuit downward from the mountain to the lake in the valley below. Little by little, his princess's death grip loosened.

"Are you afraid?"

"No! Don't stop! I love it!"

Elation shot through him, a bolt of joy lancing straight to his heart and topping all prior experiences in his life.

"Would you like to go faster?"

"Is it safe?"

"If you slip, the water will cushion your short fall."

"Then yes."

He soared low over the lake, the tip of his speared tail leaving a wake behind them as it trailed through the surface. Ana's laughter filled the air, caught by the wind, and ripped around them. Despite her earlier reservations, she maintained her seat and never lost her balance, as if she had been made to ride him. His heart swelled at the thought.

"Higher, Beast!" she cried above the wind.

"Are you certain?"

"Yes! I want to see the world from high above as you do!"

"Then hold on, my princess."

Powerful downward drafts sent them shooting up into the sky. Ana's hold on him tightened, but her excited shout assuaged his worries. Higher and higher he flew, until the air cooled and the world below them appeared minuscule. He snapped open his wings and held them outstretched, gliding across the sky.

The tension melted from her stiff and rigid posture, and without warning, his princess sprawled against his neck. She turned her cheek to his warm scales and sighed a blissful, euphoric sound. "I wish you could take me to the stars." Her words were barely more than a whisper against his neck, but he heard them as clearly as if they had seared through his soul.

And he wanted nothing more than to give them to her.

Crisp mountain air tossed Alistair's hair around his face and pulled at the tartan around his legs. The entrance to the hedge maze loomed before him, and the scent of summer flora filled the air. Wildflowers surrounded them, and night-blooming twilight roses twined over a white trellis near the entrance to the maze.

Anastasia stood beside him, her hand small and fragile within the grip of his calloused fingers. Startled, she turned her face to stare at him with wide, moss-green eyes, then tightened her fingers on his hand.

"Princess?" he whispered.

"Prince Alistair?"

He had no prior recollection of dreams resuming where their predecessors ended, but he also had no complaints if it gave him more time in a day to enjoy Anastasia's jubilant smiles, more time to hear her laughter. Whether she was a dream facsimile or not, he wanted her.

Weeks had passed since the last time she occupied his dreams, although he'd believed their newfound friendship was to blame, and that he no longer needed the phony Ana when the real one gave him affection so freely.

Is this a dream? Am I dreaming at all? he wondered.

Recovering his wits, he greeted her with a welcoming smile. "Shall we brave the labyrinth?"

"Are you certain we won't get lost?"

"There's a trick to it. A pattern," he whispered as if they might disturb someone. "Left, right, right."

The hedges rose tall around them, muting the light and the sounds from beyond the maze. A hazy green glow lit their path and pixies drifted in and out of the thick growth.

Ana kept her hand in his as they meandered at a sedate pace down the first leafy corridor. "May I ask you a question?"

"You may ask me anything," he replied. "Whether or not

I may answer is another issue altogether," he teased.

How funny that her dream self was as inquisitive as the true Anastasia.

Ana pursed her lips and slanted a studious gaze up at him. "You say 'may' as if something prevents you from speaking truthfully and openly with me," she said.

His gaze darted to her, but he said nothing. Was it possible to violate the terms of a fairy's curse while asleep? He didn't dare to trust it, and little by little, he began to doubt his ability to separate reality from fantasy.

"Is this real?"

His steps slowed, and then he stopped to hold her against his chest. It felt right there, comforting, her cheek over his wildly beating heart. "I wish that I knew," he whispered. "But I do know I'm happy with you, precious Anastasia, whether this is real or not, it changes nothing of how I feel when you are near."

Kiss me again, he tried to will her with his thoughts alone. *If this is a dream, do as I want. Kiss me.*

She didn't kiss him as she had during their previous meeting, so he seized the moment for himself and claimed her lips in a passionate kiss. She reciprocated after a startled gasp against his mouth, burying her fingers against his shoulders.

No other woman had ever felt so good in his arms. No woman had ever made his body hum with desire and come alive with desperate, burning need. He traced her curves, following the hourglass created by her corset and craving something to squeeze. In his dreams, he had arms to hold her, hands to caress and touch, and lips to kiss and enjoy the flavor of her mouth. She reminded him of ripe, sweet berries plucked fresh from the vine.

When they finally broke apart, Ana's breathy sigh against his cheek only provoked visions of her writhing beneath him in bed, her fists clutching handfuls of the sheets. He wanted more than her quiet whimpers; he wanted her pleasured cries and the sound of his name on her lips delivered in passion.

But he wanted them for real.

"This way," he murmured, taking the lead again and resuming their walk. He glanced at her pink cheeks, noting her eyes were hazy with lust, and began to doubt again. He ached for her beneath his tartan, hungering in a way kisses couldn't satisfy. Could a dream impart so many sensations and make him question reality?

Or was it a fabrication of his mind helping him to escape the brutal reality of his death looming ahead of him in a few short weeks? He dismissed it, preferring to focus on the uncomfortable tension beneath his tartan instead.

"Tell me more about Cairn Ocland," Anastasia demanded suddenly.

"What would you like to know?"

"Everything. What lies beyond it?"

Given ample distraction from his hard cock—as well as his fear of death—he chuckled and indulged her in conversation about distant lands and places he'd traveled.

"There are many places beyond Cairn Ocland's eastern borders, Princess. Savage, wild, and beautiful societies."

"I've never heard of any other kingdoms but the ones in the alliance," she said. Her brows dipped.

"The kings of Creag Morden, Liang, and Dalborough are short-sighted monarchs. They know only what they are told and see only what hovers before their faces."

"You're right."

"I am?" His brows raised.

"My father can be obstinate at the best of times, yet I still love him. Is that strange? He tried to marry me off to an awful man and abandoned me in that dismal place, but I still forgive him."

"Isn't it in the nature of children to forgive their parents' wrongdoing? They birth and nurture us, after all. We're here only by their blessing and love."

Alistair awoke, keenly aware of his huge bulk.

Only a dream, he lamented. The logs in the hearth crackled and popped, the only sound in the sleeping castle. Not even a mouse stirred

If only the true Anastasia felt for me here as she does in my dreams, the curse would be lifted and I would at last know the joys of true happiness.

Chapter 9

B EAST'S UNEXPECTED RIDE across the skies had restored an essential element to Anastasia's happiness. It had taken hours to fall asleep the previous night, and when she'd finally succumbed to physical exhaustion, she'd dreamed of her prince. Alistair dominated her sleep for the first time in weeks, catching her by surprise with a kiss so vivid she'd awakened restless with a soul-deep craving for more.

In the recent days, Beast had become strangely docile, and all hints of his former temper vanished. She couldn't remember the last time he'd raised his voice. He was her constant companion, and when her monthly time arrived, rendering her too unwell to traipse around the grounds, he chatted with her beyond the window while she curled up in bed around a hot water pouch.

When he talked, she listened, and of course, she tried to wiggle more information out of him, but some topics he still refused to touch.

Beast is hiding something. I'd love to know what mysteries he keeps from me. What is his true name? Is he perhaps the son of Queen Liadh's mount? she wondered.

The poor quality of her sleep left her groggy, and to

shake it off, she took a brisk walk in the cooling air. Their mountaintop world had transformed into shades of glorious gold and orange, and red leaves, vibrant against the stone backdrop of the castle, stretched before her. It seemed only days ago it had been summer; the time had flown by so fast.

"Princess!" Beast called from a high parapet. He scrambled down the side of the castle and loped to her like an eager pup she'd once had as a child. She giggled and turned to look up at him.

"You're certainly cheerful today, Beast."

"You give me a reason to be happy, Princess."

He escorted her to the cairn where she settled in the grass to begin her meditation, her skin tingling and abuzz with energy. For a time, she felt true peace, a sensation of being centered she'd never felt before.

When she closed her eyes, the sun was bright. They opened to the blush purple of dusk.

"Are you ready for dinner?"

"Dinner?" she asked, flabbergasted.

"Many hours have passed," Beast told her, chortling at her flustered behavior. Her eyes grew wide, and he stopped. "What is wrong?"

"You laughed. You've never laughed before."

A soft smile came over his draconic face. "Indeed. I suppose I have not, lass. Come."

"Beast?" she asked quietly after he had seated her.

"Yes, Princess?"

"Why do you never eat at the table?"

"I take my meals afterward."

"Why?"

In the time since she had become his captive, Anastasia had learned a dragon's face could become very expressive. The ridges above his ochre eyes raised, giving him a quizzical, even comical expression.

"They are too large for this table," he grumbled, unamused.

"Is your food raw? I could…." Anastasia's voice trailed, courage wavering as she decided whether or not she could handle his dietary habits. "Many cultures, even among humans, consume raw flesh. The people of Liang do. I've tried it," she declared proudly. "Father invited several of their dignitaries to Creag Morden and instructed our cooks to prepare supper in their preferred style.

"Did you like it?" he asked curiously.

"It wasn't unpleasant," she admitted. "I liked much of it, but I didn't favor the white fish filets unless they were served with rice."

The corner of his wide mouth raised, and while it would have been unperceivable to anyone else, Ana saw the tiny hint of a smile.

"Then why not dine with me," she persisted. "Whatever you eat, it doesn't matter. I feel strange sitting here across from you at this massive table while you only join me for conversation. Sometimes, I hear your belly rumbling, and I think to myself, 'He must be starved. What a spoiled arse I am to eat in front of him like this.'"

"You're not an arse if it's my preference."

"Please," she asked again.

Beast sighed. The dragon sat upon his hind legs on the floor at the end of the massive dining hall. One clawed hand raised toward his face and dropped again down to the floor. In her mind, she had the image of an exasperated man running his fingers through his hair and wondered how many of those mannerisms humans shared with higher beasts. "Once. And when it disgusts you, as it no doubt will, we'll resume our meal hours in this way."

"Deal."

He kept his word, and the next day when Ana descended the staircase, she entered the dining hall to find a table set for two. While it still appeared absurdly empty, an enormous, covered serving platter occupied his end of the table. The cook had improvised, providing him an enormous bowl of ice water beside it.

What horror waited beneath the platter? What prey did a dragon prefer, and better yet, how would he take his meal? He followed her, as usual, to pull her chair with one clawed hand. Instead of sitting, Ana studied the distance between their chairs.

"Second thoughts, lass?" he guessed.

"No. Not about this, anyway." She stacked her plates and utensils, then retraced her steps to his end of the table. The dragon followed her, the apprehensive expression on his face adding to the emotional range Ana had learned already in his company.

"What are you doing?"

"Sitting beside you."

"Why?"

"Are there other guests to join us? For what reason must I sit at the opposite end of the table, isolated and practically alone? I'd have to shout to talk to you."

"No true reason, I suppose. The table is arranged in the tradition of your homeland."

"Is this not the original dining table?"

Beast shook his head.

"I would like to see how Oclanders dine one day…. I've never favored our ways," she murmured. "Eat with me, Beast. Please," she pleaded.

"As you wish," he said in a quiet voice.

Ana managed not to flinch when Beast unveiled his dinner. Steam rose from the seared flesh, but the succulent aroma made her mouth water.

"My meal has revolted you," he stated. With his claw, he recovered the roasted boar with the lid.

"No! Far from it. It smells delightful," Ana said. She rose and placed her hand atop one of his huge talons and nudged. "Please uncover it again. Did you do this yourself, or is there an oven within this castle large enough to bake such a monstrous hog?"

"I did," he confessed.

"May I cut a portion for myself to accompany my supper?"

He lowered to his haunches again and gestured with an extended claw. He gazed upon her with wonder in his eyes, as well as skepticism when Ana sliced into the unfortunate creature with the knife she'd used for her roast pheasant.

A more squeamish princess would have turned her head when Beast lowered his head and ripped the first shreds of meat from his dinner. She watched instead, deliberately focused on the way his teeth closed around the flank.

I will not shame him for being who he is. I won't look away.

A bone crunched between his massive teeth. She answered by raising her wine chalice for a sip. Through virtue of willpower and affection for him, she sliced into the crispy flesh on her own plate. The taste was rich, smoky and flavorful, a hint of expected game, but nothing offensive to her palate. She glanced up to see him watching her closely.

"It's good."

"It is?" His heavy brows shot up so high she thought they'd take flight. She giggled at the imagery.

"I enjoy it very much and hope you'll prepare another tomorrow."

"I will." Lowering his chin and directing an intense, focused gaze to her face, Beast spoke the question she had come to expect during their supper. "Do you think you could love a beast such as me?"

Each day, he prepared her another meal, another creature to share together, and each day he asked her some variety of his original inquiry.

Could she love him? Did she feel affection for him?

The questions didn't end, but they no longer frightened her. Perhaps he needed reassurance of her happiness.

And if it was that simple, she couldn't fault him at all.

"I feel friendship," Ana told him by the third month of her pseudo-captivity. She sat on the balcony attached to her bedroom, its view overlooking the courtyard.

"Friendship?" Beast asked. While standing on all fours on the level terrain outside, the dragon's face was even with the balcony.

"A close friendship with someone who has treated me well and given me anything I could see in even my fondest dreams. You've given me everything but the stars."

"Perhaps I should give you those too."

Chapter 10

GENTLE, STEADY RAIN forced Ana to remain indoors as a turbulent and gray cloud cover spanned from one horizon to the next. Initially, she had considered guiding the storm away or attempting to disperse it, but a passage in the Witch Queen's weather tome had advised against unnecessarily disturbing the natural state of the world. It cautioned young witches to respect nature.

What good was such power if she couldn't use it to her benefit? She read the passage again and asked Beast, who had chuckled again in his rich baritone. She loved his laughter and wanted to hear more of it.

"In Cairn Ocland, the spirits of the skies, wind, water, and earth are our gods," the dragon had replied.

Which had promptly set her to fretting about practicing with the storm magic, certain she'd offended some goddess until he assured her magic used in study wasn't the same as arrogance.

So as days passed, Ana came to appreciate the frequent storms and heavy rain, but she continued to yearn for the countryside's warm breeze. She especially missed charging across the plains with Sterling. How was her gentle mare?

She could only hope Victoria stepped up in her absence and devoted the grooming care her dear friend deserved.

Due to the unforgiving weather, Beast was also forced indoors. He joined her in the dining room, though he had declined breakfast and curled beside the large hearth fire instead to warm his scarlet hide.

"You dislike the rain, don't you?"

"It is not my favorite," he grumbled. "Have you ever seen a dragon sneeze? It is not fun."

Giggling, she imagined each sneeze accompanied by a jet of fire.

"But I do like the rain at times. There are no tubs large enough for a dragon, you see, lass, so I have to make do with what I can find."

"There's the lake," she pointed out

"Aye, and it'll be frigid in a month or two." He stretched on the stone floor with a groan.

"Would you be more comfortable on a carpet?"

"Anything is better than this floor, but this fire is the largest in the castle."

"Then come with me to the library," Anastasia urged him.

"What use would I have there among the many books?" Beast asked, bewildered.

"It's warm, for one. You can read with me."

Beast snorted. Twin plumes of white smoke exited the dragon's nostrils, and he grumbled an irritated noise of discontent. "I cannot."

"Why not?"

"My claws are too large for books."

"Oh. For a moment, I thought you planned to say you couldn't read."

Beast said nothing, but the truth was in his expression.

"You can't read," she whispered. "I'm sorry, I should have realized." After all, how would a dragon learn to read human books?

"Och, no. I can read." He sighed, and the warmth of his breath stirred her hair, blowing strands around her face. He smelled like smoke and familiar things skimming the edge of her memory, almost masculine.

What a silly thought to have, she chided herself, embarrassed. He was a man. A male dragon, but technically a man among his species.

"Not well?" she asked.

Beast nodded.

Sensing the dragon's embarrassment, Ana cupped her palm against his scaled cheek. "Then I will read to you. Please, come with me. The doors are large enough. I'm positive it's one of the few rooms in this castle able to hold you."

Beast gave her an uncertain look, but he followed without further complaint. Their path led up the stairs and into the library where she propped open the heavy doors with a pair of ornate wedges. Everything about Benthwaite Castle was beautiful, from the intricately designed stairway railings to the door stops designed to resemble vines. She sighed at the beauty, and Beast laughed at her.

"Of all the things to admire in this castle, you choose the wedges for the door."

"I can't help it. They're beautiful and I never noticed it before."

"There are many things in this castle you've never noticed."

"Too true. I find it more breathtaking with each passing day, like a mystery to unravel." She flounced into the room and twirled near the center of the floor, skirts spinning around her legs. "Come join me, Beast! There's plenty of room, see?"

He prowled forward, and with his wings folded against his body, he cleared the wide double doors with ease.

"Much time has passed since I stepped beyond these doors," he murmured.

Were those tears in his eyes? He turned in a circle to view the entire floor, with its wall-to-ceiling rows of shelves and upper level accessible by stairs.

Just who was he to the Witch Queen and her mount? Curiouser and curiouser, she began to form her own speculations. He had to be the great dragon's son, perhaps the lone survivor of King Frederick's siege.

"I have found many books here, from fiction to gnomish science. What would you like to hear?" she asked.

"I would enjoy any story spoken from your lips," Beast said.

Chuckling, she ran her fingers over the assortment of

VIVIENNE SAVAGE

favorites she'd collected from the shelves over the course of many weeks' visits. She kept them close at hand to read on a whim. Finding tomes written in her native tongue had been surprisingly easy, the library a match of both languages.

"Romance or a little mystery? I translated this Langese love story with a lingual charm. Beast? What is your native tongue?"

"Oclander," he replied.

"Yet you know my language, too. Why is that?"

He shrugged. "Know thy enemy, for knowledge is the way to his destruction," he recited.

"Is that the only reason?"

"Dalborough has long haunted this kingdom. We learned their language, and by proxy, yours as well, so that we would know the evil our enemies speak to us before we removed their tongues."

She shivered. "Romance, it is," she muttered to herself. Beast overheard her and laughed.

In a clear voice, she read aloud from the storybook while her dragon curled beside the fireplace on his stomach, his chin resting over the top of his claws. Whenever she lifted her gaze from the pages, she found him devoted to her words and watching with all of his attention.

By the second hour, she desired a glass of water. To her surprise, or perhaps not even to her surprise anymore, she saw a glass beside her on the table.

"It's magic, isn't it? This is an enchanted castle," Ana said.

"It is," Beast confirmed. "Though it only took you *months* to notice."

She scrunched her nose in response to his teasing. He'd become more open and playful over the recent weeks as their friendship progressed. "I had convinced myself it was Hora tiptoeing around the halls, but I suppose I've known all along it couldn't be her. I've read of these so many times in fairy tales but never believed I would enter one." She sipped the sweet spring water and resumed their story.

Beast interrupted her for the first time as they neared the end of the tale. She had abandoned her seat at the table to sit beside him on the carpet with her legs folded beneath her.

"Do you believe in such things?"

"Which?" she asked.

"True love's kiss."

Anastasia contemplated his question. "My mother and father were truly in love. Were yours?"

"Very much. But a kiss did not save them."

"I'm sorry," she whispered.

He shook his head. "It happened many years ago and is no fault of yours, Princess. Please, finish your story."

Ana set the book aside and leaned forward to place a hand on his face. "We can stop if it's bringing up bad memories."

"You didn't make me sad, Anastasia. Memories did," he told her in a gentle voice. His eyes closed as she splayed her fingers over his cheek. Heat radiated from the glossy scales, and they truly did resemble fire captured in flakes of amber.

"And sometimes, memories are all I have."

"You have me." Startled, amber and green eyes opened to dart to her face. She caressed the ridge above his eye and smiled. "You're my friend, Beast. Maybe the best friend I've had in a long while besides my cousin Victoria."

"Me?"

"You listen to me."

He blinked and said nothing while Ana watched her own reflection in his enormous eyes. She stroked his nose again. "And you've never hurt me."

"I never will." His eyes drifted to the window where the storm had broken, revealing patches of starry sky between intermittent wisps of cloud. Abruptly standing, Beast stretched out his long body and shifted his tail over the carpeted floor. "Let us save the rest of the tale for another day. I wish to show you something new."

"Where?"

"It's a secret. You're not allowed to know until we arrive so you must close your eyes." She crinkled her nose, and after a moment, the dragon continued with an amused, "Your face will freeze that way."

"You sound like my mother," she grumbled. "I do not like surprises."

"You've liked the others, and you will like this one." Beast tilted his head and gazed at her with gentle eyes. "Do I still have your trust, Princess?"

The question took her by surprise, but when she looked

into his green, gold-flecked eyes, she saw only sincerity. A strange sense in the back of her mind told her to speak. "Yes."

With her eyes closed, Beast guided her up the castle stairs to the next level. He walked on all fours, and she felt the occasional nudge of his snout against her shoulder. His warm breath rustled her hair, tickling her neck, and she giggled as she felt in front of her.

"This way," he encouraged her.

They ascended another flight, and then another. She counted and furrowed her brow when she realized they were heading to the forbidden upper level.

"Here," Beast said. His claws, warm to the touch, guided her hand to a banister.

One more flight. The fifth floor. A door creaked open and the cold breeze rushed inside against her cheeks.

"Now you may look," he said.

Ana opened her eyes to the sight of a round chamber with multiple windows. A giant brass telescope dominated the center of the room, positioned on a raised platform and angled out the northern window

"This is... it's an astronomy tower!" she cried gleefully. "You said you would give me the stars one day and you did it!"

"The telescope rotates," Beast told her in a quiet voice. When he squeezed in behind her and wiggled the front of his body into the space, his sides scraped against the inside of the open doors. Where he touched, the stone around the threshold gleamed. Either Alistair or another dragon before him had worn it smooth.

"The stars are so clear here in the mountains, and this will bring them even closer. Oh, I wish you could look, too."

Her dragon couldn't get his wings past the door.

"Seeing your happiness is enough," Beast replied. "Each of the windows are hinged. The Storm King, father of the Witch Queen, favored this room and spared no expense in its construction. Stories say he would spend hours here each day and that the scope is enchanted to see beyond the range of any mundane magnifying instrument. He knew whenever there were troubles in his villages, with bandits or invaders, and would fly upon the clouds themselves to resolve dilemmas."

Blinking didn't alleviate the burning sensation behind her eyelids. "I don't know what to say. Thank you doesn't feel adequate. It's amazing! It's—I can't find words to tell you how wonderful this is, Beast."

Ana threw herself at the dragon and found the perfect spot to hold him, her body pressed in the groove between his neck and shoulder.

"You could always marry me," Beast offered playfully.

Ana giggled and caressed the ridges on his snout. "If I could marry any dragon, it would probably be you," she whispered. "Thank you, Beast."

"Disregard anything I may have said about the fourth floor, princess. You may come and go as you please. This is your home, and at home, you shall know only peace."

For the second time, her dream of Alistair resumed where the last encounter had ended. She found the continuity odd, having never experienced such a thing before. Beside her, the dream prince appeared equally puzzled, but then he smiled and cupped her cheeks between his hands.

"Are you ready to see the heart of the maze, my lass?"

"Is it close?"

"Aye, only around this last bend. I promised I would see you through."

"We're not there yet," she teased.

Laughing, her prince released her and took her hand, giving a gentle tug as he led the way. An unidentifiable source of illumination shone ahead of them through the hedges, emitting an azure light spreading toward the heavens. Her heart skipped with enthusiasm, thrumming a wild rhythm behind her ribs.

For all of the time she had lived in the castle, she'd never asked Beast to lead her to the center of the labyrinth. It felt too personal, something shared between her and the dream prince alone, and she'd been too shy to mention the matter of her nighttime adventures with her daylight companion.

"And we've reached the center." Alistair bowed and swept his arm out. "As promised."

Her imagination had constructed an elaborate place of unearthly beauty with a natural hot spring bubbling in the

  VIVIENNE SAVAGE

center, large enough for two to enjoy in comfort. Stone lanterns and magnificent statues of fairies occupied each corner, the winged women poised as if they were about to take flight. Lush clover blanketed the ground, dotted with wildflowers in bold red, soft purple, and golden yellow.

"Oh Alistair, it's lovely."

"It pales in comparison to you, beautiful Anastasia."

She turned, releasing her hold on his arm in favor of setting both hands against his chest. "I promised you a reward."

His eyes lit with desire. She sighed as he stroked her waist, his hands following the outline of her body until both palms cupped her hips and eased around to squeeze two handfuls of her bottom. "Only what you wish to give."

Her dream. Her choices.

Ana chose boldness and gave in to her desires. Spreading the opening of his shirt, she leaned in and pressed her lips over his heart, tasting his warm, golden skin.

Under the moonlight, she felt confident and courageous. Unstoppable. She had become the mistress of her own dream, guiding her desires to the outcome she craved. If she wanted a bath with a handsome young man, no one would be the wiser.

"Turn around," she whispered before kissing his lips again.

Questioning brows raised, and then he complied as she'd bid him and turned his back. With him facing away, she shed her clothes and hurried to the spring. Hot water embraced her, the perfect temperature to sink into up to her shoulder beneath the cloudless sky.

"Will you join me?" she called.

Alistair turned. His gaze found her piled clothes first, then drifted to her in the pool. He seemed to freeze in place, his only movement the flare of his nostrils.

"Well?" she called again. "Will you join me, my prince?"

Unlike her, Alistair didn't ask her to turn around as he undressed. He shrugged off his shirt and dropped his hands to his heavy belt. Barely tearing her eyes away in time to focus on the water, she heard the heavy thump of his belt hitting the grass. She imagined the tartan unwinding and the bare skin it would reveal. Swallowing, she sank deeper in the spring.

Heat rose into her cheeks. Dream or not, she struggled against years of modest upbringing. What if it wasn't a dream? She didn't dare to ask him, frightened she'd shatter the illusion and her prince would vanish forever.

As she debated the possibilities of his existence, Alistair crossed the distance between them and joined her in the pool, not stopping until he stood right beside her. She swallowed.

"Is this what you wished?" he asked.

Words failed her, and all she could do was nod, which brought a smile to her prince's mouth. He stepped in closer, nudging their bodies together.

Steam curled up through the air, but the damp heat held no comparison to the warmth pooling in her belly. Everywhere their bodies touched, her skin felt on fire, even beneath the water—especially beneath the water.

VIVIENNE SAVAGE

"I promised you everything." She found her voice and skimmed her hands up his chest to his neck. Her lips settled over the pulse point at his throat then eagerly climbed upward, only to linger at his jaw. Alistair groaned and turned his head, capturing her lips.

He ignited a spark within Ana. Her gut clenched, and her toes curled against the mossy bottom of the spring. Instinctively, her arms tightened around his shoulders, and she rose to tiptoe, pressing her bare breasts against his chest. Her nipples skimmed against hard muscle and slick skin, their nudity concealed under the cover of night with only the ghostly, pale blue glow of the stone lanterns in each corner of the maze's center.

The hot, unyielding length of him brushed her hip. She gasped in surprise, and then he coaxed her lips to part. What began as sweet became passionate and searing, hungrily tasting then stroking inside her mouth with his tongue. Where Edward had forced, Alistair coaxed, gentle but no less impassioned.

"Make love to me," she pleaded on a breathless exhale.

His strong hands skimmed down her bare back and cupped her bottom. Excitement mingled with panic, anticipation with nervousness. His erection pressed into her softer skin, wedged against her belly.

But he made no move to join them together.

"Alist—"

He cut her off with another kiss. "Not yet, my love."

"Not yet?" she asked, bewildered. Had her dream man just denied her sex? She blinked up at him. "Have I done something wrong?"

"No," he murmured. "Believe me, Anastasia, you've done everything right. But it would be wrong of me, and dishonorable to claim you as mine now. Not while I'm a captive here." He raised her hand from the water and kissed her knuckles without removing his eyes from her face.

"I don't understand. Captive? Then that means… this isn't…?"

"This is no normal dream. I've realized that now. All along I was uncertain, but now I see the truth."

Not a dream. If it wasn't a dream, then it meant a real man stood before her, a flesh and blood man inhabiting her personal fantasies and most private thoughts. In one moment, she wanted to leap away from him and shield her nudity, but in the next, she yielded to the new, salacious and bold side of her personality. Fearless, her fingers glided low and curled around the thick, hard shaft between them.

A low growl rumbled in Alistair's chest. The forward thrust of his hips elicited a surge of satisfaction, prompting her to stroke again. "Tell me how to rescue you," she whispered against his throat.

"I… I can't," he moaned. The hand cupping her bottom squeezed harder. "You've already come so close, lass. Open your eyes. I cannot tell you anything more."

"Why not? Why can't you tell me more?"

VIVIENNE SAVAGE

"I've told you everything I can."

Anastasia startled awake in her bed. She jerked up into a half-seated position with her eyes wide open. Strands of red hair clung to her cheeks, and she groaned when the morning sun shone across her face.

Her chest heaved, but there was no sign of Prince Alistair beside her or in the room at all, once again leading her to wonder if the magnificent specimen of royalty was a figment of her imagination. Perhaps her inner psyche created another human to fulfill something Beast lacked.

"Or if not a dream, then perhaps a warning and a plea for help…. If he is here and a captive in this castle, I must find him. Yes. I shall."

The princess untangled the sheets from her ankles and legs then tossed them aside. Her thin night rail clung to her curves, the cotton semi-translucent with sweat. As usual, a prepared bath awaited her. She no longer questioned it after so many weeks in the castle.

All the while that she soaked, her mind furiously worked at untangling the mystery of the hidden prince's cryptic words. She stepped from the tub and dried herself with haste before she chose the first gown that came to her hand.

"What does he mean, open my eyes?" she demanded of the empty room. "What am I missing?"

I'm not a captive, she told herself. Beast was her friend, yet fleeting moments of yearning demanded the company of other humans. She missed the late night conversations with

Beauty & the Beast 174

her cousin Victoria, their mischief making in Lorehaven, and afternoon tea over pastries. There would be no more soft butter cookies on spring afternoons with jasmine tea while they discussed boys and exchanged gossip.

But she was no captive. She'd accepted her fate of her own free will. If Alistair was imprisoned, she'd have to make Beast answer for it and set the prince free.

"Maybe he truly isn't aware that there's another survivor," she said aloud. "Perhaps he would be as thrilled as I am. After all, there are places in this castle where he cannot go."

What secrets did the castle conceal, and how much of it did Beast know?

If Alistair had been confined to a room in the castle, then she would find him.

She moved from one corridor to the next during her search, opening doors and peering into vacant, disused bedrooms for overlooked clues. When she reached the once-forbidden fourth floor, an electric jolt buzzed over her skin and raised every fine hair on her arms.

Here was where she'd find her answers. She passed landscape watercolors and portraits of unfamiliar, red-haired monarchs dressed in furs, leathers, and the same green tartan pattern Alistair had worn.

How could she have dreamed up such a pattern with perfect accuracy? Had she seen it in a history book perhaps? Her belly sank, and nervous butterflies took flight within it as she advanced down the corridor. Each step echoed, and at any moment, she thought Beast would thunder into the hall and find her snooping despite his previous day's decision to grant her access to the entire castle.

"Alistair?" she called in a loud whisper, too afraid to shout.

She opened another door and found a bedroom. Unlike others she had come across, this one held a variety of personal objects, and clothes were laid out over the bed. A gleaming sword with dragons etched into the blade leaned against the footboard. Its blade stretched nearly as long as she stood tall. Imagining it in Alistair's hands, she smiled and ran her fingers over the cool metal. It had to be his. The room smelled like him, and although he wasn't there with her, his sense of presence remained, like a ghost lingering over her shoulder, like he'd been there but she arrived moments too late to catch him.

Was he a ghost, a trapped spirit awaiting freedom from the past?

She hoped not, praying she'd find him alive.

The next room projected a similar sensation of occupancy, though it was as vacant as all the chambers before it. The hearth glowed hot and bright like every other room with a fireplace in the castle. A small, round table with three chairs sat a short distance away from the flames. Gold-rimmed plates, ornately fashioned silverware, and crystal goblets occupied each place setting.

"This must be where the royal family took their meals

together."

Beast had told her the Oclanders preferred intimate family settings over the impersonal dining halls of the western kingdoms.

The hearth sparked, an ember leaping out from the fireplace onto the stone. She glanced at it again, and then her breath caught in her throat.

She found him.

Above the mantle, an exquisite oil painting depicted three people. A statuesque woman with waist-length, ginger hair stood beside an equally tall, dark-haired man. His strong jaw and strange, golden eyes struck her as familiar. Between them, a boy on the cusp of manhood leaned against the woman's side, and a strong familial resemblance told her the boy was their son. He had the same nose and squared face as his father, but his mother's fair coloring.

It was the same face she'd seen in her dreams, albeit years younger, no older than twelve or thirteen.

"Alistair," Anastasia whispered. The discovery became her motivation to resume a feverish search of the upper level. Being in his home made her feel closer to him, a man who existed somewhere beyond her mind. A man who needed her and depended on her help.

But no matter where she looked or how long she searched, Anastasia found no sign of the lost prince. He may as well have been a figment of her imagination, after all.

Chapter 11

"A NA COULD BE the one, Alistair. What will you do if she's the one able to break your curse and restore your humanity?" Hora asked. She drifted in the breeze, an ethereal blur of muted colors beneath the afternoon sun.

"I don't know," he admitted. "Miss you, perhaps. Rejoice that my life isn't over. Try to live up to the standard my parents have set as rulers to this kingdom." He sighed. "Restore Ocland."

Hora chuckled and raised her face toward the sky. "Sometimes when I stand like this, it's almost as if I'm alive again."

"I wish you were alive again. There are few things I wouldn't give to keep you here with me always, Nan."

"Don't fib, little one. You were long adjusted to my being gone when Eos created this curse. Though I've appreciated every moment in this strange, counterfeit excuse for a life."

"You're right. But I will always miss you. If only I knew what to do about Anastasia. My heart tells me I must release her from our bloodpact if we're ever to have true love, but my mind... my mind fears death. There are mere days left to me. What if it isn't enough time?"

"She loves you, Alistair. Perhaps the girl hasn't said it, but she does. I see it in the way she looks at you each day. You're comfortable with each other."

Alistair growled. "Comfort isn't love."

"I once changed your diapers, little one. Your growls mean nothing to me. Look, as I see it, the girl's captivity ceased many weeks ago, and she has since become a guest—a protected guest who is practically a member of the household. She has nowhere to go and enjoys your company." Hora touched his chest, splaying her fingers over the scales above his heart. "Tell her what she means to you, beyond the curse, but deep inside here."

"I do not want to lose her, Hora. What if you are wrong? What if she desires freedom more than me? Eos has played a dangerous game by tangling our dreams together, but what Ana loves is a human body I may never have."

"Anastasia has a kind heart," the ghost disagreed. "Trust in her to see the clues Eos has woven between you. Now seek her out and do as your heart tells you. Are you a chicken or a dragon?"

He chuckled quietly and rose to his clawed feet.

"A chicken would be braver. I should know. I was once chased by them as a cub."

The setting sun turned the sky into a canvas painted with watercolors. Pink, lilac, and golden-orange washed across

  VIVIENNE SAVAGE

the horizon. Sometimes, she missed the world below the mountain, and at other times, the castle felt like the home she'd enjoyed as a little girl. The safe haven her father destroyed by handing her over to Dalborough's royal family.

Beast trudged into view from the eastern castle grounds, his flank ruby in the dwindling light.

"There you are!" Ana cried. She set aside the cup of chamomile and rose from her seat. He met her at the balcony rail with what she'd come to think of as a grin on his draconic face. The expression showed his teeth, but it never frightened her. If anything, she felt comforted by knowing her kind host was in high spirits.

"Apologies for my tardiness," he rumbled. "Hora felt I was in need of her counsel, so I've come with news."

"Oh? About what?"

He shook his head shyly, but the same hint of a toothy smile remained. "What occupied your day?" he asked, practicing the usual redirection to divert focus back on her.

"I… I explored the fourth floor."

The sound of her racing heart nearly drowned out Beast's muted, "Ah." His good humor faded, but the dragon didn't raise his voice or accuse her of trespassing. He only looked upon her with somber eyes. "And what, dear princess, did you discover?"

"I like the dinner table," she told him.

Beast chuckled, a soft and short-lived sound.

"Could there be someone else here, Beast?" she said in

a rush, gathering her courage. "Someone you know nothing about since most of the castle is inaccessible to you, I mean."

"There is no one else, Princess. No one. No one currently lives in this castle but the two of us."

"But there's Hora."

He didn't answer.

"Beast, would you permit me to look at the dungeons? I tried the door a few moments ago, but it requires a key."

"Anastasia, there is no one below, in this you have my word and solemn vow. The dungeons are not safe and no place for you to be. It is a foul place without light or life where many soldiers of Dalborough saw their last days."

"Oh." She deflated and dropped her shoulders, sighing. If Beast knew there were no people in the dungeon, then she believed him. She trusted him.

"Do you think you could love a beast like me, Anastasia?"

He hadn't asked the question in days, if not weeks. She couldn't recall the last time he'd voiced the strange, albeit pitiful inquiry. It tugged her heart, and this time, her eyes burned with tears when she answered. "Yes. I love you very much, Beast."

Her dragon's eyes grew large, and she realized he was holding his breath, as if waiting for something. When nothing happened, a frown overtook his face. "I see. Then you are free."

"Of course I'm free," she said, laughing. "I've never been made to feel like a prisoner."

"No, I mean…." Beast huffed, the warm plume of air

VIVIENNE SAVAGE

ruffling the hem of her dress. "I am setting you free, Anastasia. Free to return home and take your mother the flower she needs. Free to live your life however you choose."

His words struck her, a verbal lance to her heart. They fell over Ana with the same shock as a bucket of cold water, dousing the effervescent mood inspired by discovering her prince wasn't a product of her lonely mind's need for human companionship.

"What if I do not wish to leave?"

"You must. You deserve more than this lonely mountain, my beautiful Anastasia. You deserve your family and your friends. You deserve a chance to find love."

Anastasia tucked her chin toward her chest, only for the blunt side of his index claw to nudge her. The tender touch and his obvious concern blurred her vision with tears.

"But what will you do, Beast? You'll be all alone."

Beast watched her. For the first time in weeks since their initial meeting, she couldn't read his expressions and pick up the subtle nuances in the way his brow ridges dipped or his eyes narrowed. "I do not yet know."

"You no longer want me," she whispered.

His expression remained unchanged, face carved from stone. "That is where you are wrong. I have come to love you as well... and I realize now, imprisonment is never the answer to love."

"When must I go?"

"Tomorrow," he said in his soft rumble. "The snow will

begin to fall soon, and you will have a long ride ahead of you."

"Ride? I have no horse, Beast. Couldn't you fly me? Then the trip will be less than a day and I can remain longer."

Beast shook his head. "No. I have sworn never to enter your kingdom again, and I will honor that oath."

Anastasia narrowed her eyes. "No! You promised to never do harm there again. I know our oath, Beast." He'd lied to her. For the first time, as far as she could tell, her dragon had lied.

"This is how it must be. Farewell, Anastasia." The stoic facade failed as emotion seeped into his glossy eyes. His voice cracked as he turned tail and uttered a final, "Goodbye," before rushing away.

The hasty retreat contradicted everything she knew of the straightforward dragon. She pursed her lips, but before she could respond, he vanished around the corner of the castle.

VIVIENNE SAVAGE

Chapter 12

THE FAIRY HAD lied to him. Ana confessed her love, but his ability to shift never returned. And without the ability to shift, the ax hovering above his head also remained. He was a man doomed to die, a mere day from the anniversary of his curse.

"How could you do this to me, Eos?" he cried to the open skies, loathing her for the deception. "You betrayed me! You gave me hope all this time of achieving humanity again, and robbed me of it!"

Had she set him up all along for failure as a cruel joke?

Expressing mutual love for Anastasia had changed nothing, and he felt no shift in the magic binding him to his dragon form. He'd paced the castle grounds for an hour attempting to transform, only to feel a crushing weight holding him in place.

Letting Ana go was the only thing left he could do. He refused to let her watch him die. Refused to leave her abandoned and alone to waste away in what would become a decrepit ruin after the enchantment broke and cold winter arrived.

How long, he wondered, would it take for Benthwaite to

be forgotten from all memory? Eventually, one of the kings would send another pack of treasure hunters to plunder the crumbling skeleton of his ancestral home, and once it was thoroughly gutted, they would slam the final nail in a once proud culture's coffin.

"All I can do is see her safely away, with the means to live her life however she chooses."

As if to add insult to injury, a cloudless day dawned, the sun casting golden rays to every window-filled castle corridor. A final day of faux summer warmth before winter dug in its claws and covered the mountains in ice and snow. Ana readied herself with reluctance, taking her time while soaking in every detail about her room. She didn't want to forget a single thing about the only time in her life when she'd felt truly free.

"I'll have to come back," she muttered to herself. "No matter what he says. Once the spring thaw comes, I'll ride back up here. I *will* find my way."

Although she had no appetite for breakfast, she'd forced down tea and a few bites of toast and jam with honey. Beast didn't join her. She lingered at the table, hoping he would arrive, realizing he mattered more than a lost ghost in a forlorn castle. The mission to rescue her dream prince lost its meaning, and if given a choice between discovering his whereabouts or keeping her dragon, she'd choose Beast every time.

Hora met her at the stairs with tears in her sorrowful blue

VIVIENNE SAVAGE

eyes. "I wish you the very best, Anastasia."

"I don't want to go."

"Oh, my dear, I know, but some things are… well, they're meant to be as they are. He only wants what's best for you."

Ana sighed. It seemed everyone always wanted what was best for her, but no one cared what she wanted.

"I'll miss you, Hora."

"And you will be missed, Anastasia. You brought sunlight and happiness to this old castle, and joy that can never be forgotten. Thank you."

Dipping forward to embrace the older woman, her arms closed around empty air instead and passed through a formless apparition. Ana jerked back, startled by the cool sensation against her skin. Stumbling back, her wide-eyed stare landed on Hora's wavering, semi-translucent form.

"You're a ghost!"

"Think of me as the spirit of the castle. I have been here for a very long time." Hora smiled, unflustered by her shock.

A war of emotions took place within her, despair overwhelmed by a bolt of optimism. "Then if you are a ghost, tell me of Prince Alistair. Please, Hora, is he dead as well? I've dreamed of him several times since arriving at this castle. Is there any way I may save him?"

The old woman shook her head. "I fear there is no saving our prince and he's forever lost, Anastasia. Go now and enjoy life, for there is none here in this castle, lass. This is a place of death."

Tears welled beneath her lashes as her final bubble of hope burst, the crushing reality of her failure in its place. There was no prince, and Beast no longer desired her company. Everyone who had come to mean something to Ana had abandoned her.

"Goodbye, Hora. Thank you for everything."

"Be well, my dear."

She walked through the silent halls, each step toward the front door adding to her turmoil, weights stacked atop an already heavy heart. It seemed almost as if the castle went dim behind her, lights snuffing out and rooms going cold.

Anastasia suppressed the reluctance to leave her new home behind and emerged from the castle, feeling cold and sick in her stomach. A saddled, gray horse awaited her, packed for her journey.

"Sterling?"

The impossible had occurred. Unable to believe her eyes, Ana stood anchored to the spot until the mare trotted over and bumped her velvety nose against her rider's chest in greeting.

"But how…?"

Beast moved into her field of vision. "You required a mount. The castle provided. It seems fitting you should have a friend to see you safely home."

"I wish that friend were you, Beast. Please come with me. We'll take the flower to my father together. We'll make him see reason. Or we can leave it there and travel elsewhere if you've grown tired of this mountain. Think of the places we can see and visit together. Only the two of us."

VIVIENNE SAVAGE

Beast shook his head. "I cannot leave the place of my birth."

"You've left plenty of times to set fire to our kingdoms!" she protested.

"This is different, Anastasia."

Peering into his eyes, she saw the dishonesty beneath and knew he was hiding something from her.

"You are lying to me. What have I done that my best friend lies to me so freely?"

"It is not a lie, Princess. In time, perhaps, you will come to understand. Here. Here is the flower to save your mother."

Beast opened one curled claw to reveal two roses nestled within his grasp. Their petals faded from deep violet at their tips to a soft lavender at the base, the leaves and stems dark green and spiked with golden-tipped thorns.

"Brew tea with the dried petals of one flower, and your mother shall be cured."

"And the second rose?"

"For you, should you ever come to need it. They are the final two roses of autumn, and no more shall bloom until spring. If at all." His morose voice broke her heart.

Ana took the offered flowers and wrapped them in a silk handkerchief, too overwhelmed by emotions to offer more than a choked, "Thank you."

"I have one final gift to give you, Princess."

"You've given me enough, Beast. What more could you have to offer?"

"This staff was once used by the Witch Queen, and is all that remains of her. It's my gift to you, and may it always keep you safe in your travels."

Ana stared up at him. In his clawed hand, the staff resembled the world's most ornate toothpick, carved from white wood and affixed with cherry red jewels. Each gem twinkled like red starlight against the shadows created by the overhang above the castle entrance. The head of it glittered with gold, and a foot-long blade gleamed with a diamond edge.

"Take it," Beast insisted again, nudging it against her chest.

"I… you kept the Witch Queen's staff?"

"Yes. Please take it. She would want it to be held by a woman of pure heart with a clean soul. A woman like you. Do this for me, Ana."

He'd never shortened her name before. The urgency in his voice tugged at her memories, something about his tone and inflection striking her as familiar.

"You called me Ana," she whispered.

"So I did."

Almost afraid to take it into her possession, she reached out and curled her fingers around the mystical relic of a woman long dead. It flashed with light, power flaring within each jewel on contact, and then it surged down the ivory shaft until it radiated energy.

"I couldn't take this from you, Beast. The Witch Queen clearly meant a lot to you, and if I leave with it, you'll never get it back."

"I do not want it back. I want your safety. I want…." He struggled to conceal his longing behind a stony expression, towering above her from his lofty stance on all fours.

Her eyes burned, tears bubbling at the edge of her vision, but she took the staff and turned away. "Then I will do as you've bid me. Good day, Beast. Perhaps I may visit one day—"

"No," he simply said. "You must never return, Anastasia. There is a life for you beyond this mountain, a good life, a charmed life."

"I want to stay here to be with you, Beast."

He shook his head and backed away from her. "No. That is no longer possible, my sweet princess." Without looking at her, he turned his back to her, revealing massive wings and his immense tail.

"I don't regret it. I don't regret a single day of our friendship."

The enormous dragon chuckled dryly. "Neither do I."

He left her alone in the courtyard, surrounded by chirping birds.

Darkness. Thick clouds blotted out the moon and the stars above her. Even the lanterns had been extinguished, the only light emitted by fireflies flying in lazy circles around the hot spring.

"Alistair?"

She rushed to the still body lying against the clover and dropped to her knees beside him, dread heavy in her heart.

"Ana?" His eyes blinked open, dull against his pale face. "Ana, you should not be here. You should be home."

"What's happened to you?"

He tried to smile up at her, but his expression faltered. "What must happen."

"I don't understand."

"My sweet, sweet princess." He lifted his hand to her face and cupped her cheek. "From the moment I first saw you, your bravery awed me. I need you to hold onto that bravery and strength now."

"You speak as though I'll never see you again." But this was her dream, and he couldn't die in her dream. She refused to allow it. "I'll return. I'll find a magician or sorceress to help find you...."

"No. You must never return here." His intense gaze bored into her. "Go home. Begin anew."

"Alis—"

His fingers pressed against her lips.

"I have made peace with my fate. Go, my beautiful Ana. Live a happy life, the one you deserve, full of light, laughter, and love. May my mother's staff serve you well."

Ana woke, unsettled by the strange dream. Despite the charmed cloak tucked close around her body, a deep chill settled in her limbs.

"I will come back," she whispered to the empty mountain

  VIVIENNE SAVAGE

as she lay down once more. She slept restlessly, but dreamlessly, tossing and turning on her bedroll, and awakened before the dawn. Sterling nickered in greeting and scraped the dew dampened grass with a hoof.

"Rough night for you as well?"

Her limbs creaked as she rose and stretched, stiff from a night on the hard ground after months in a bed soft as a cloud. She missed the castle already.

When she had stopped for the night, she'd discovered one saddle bag was packed to the brim with food and drink for her journey, far too much to be contained by so small a satchel. The other contained clothes, the dresses and outfits she had favored during her stay. But beneath the colorful layers, she'd uncovered massive quantities of gold and silver coins, immeasurable, seemingly endless wealth.

Beast had sent her away with a hoard, from coins to gemstones and glittering jewelry.

"Are you ready to go home, Sterling?" Ana saddled her mare after packing up camp. "Of course, you've been home all this time, haven't you? Still, I'm glad you're here."

Ana led the way on foot, too restless to wait for sunrise but unwilling to risk riding the treacherous trail in the dark. Around the next turn, the view opened up. In the valley below, a hundred fires twinkled like distant stars.

Her heart lurched in her chest. "Oh no. No, no, no," Ana breathed.

The first faint hints of color tinged the sky, illuminating

the black banners waving over the army camped below.

Was this the second test Eleanor had mentioned that day in the woods? She'd put her life on the line for Beast a dozen times. Anything else was out of the question.

"We have to let Beast know Dalborough has come for him."

Her beautiful, smart and sassy horse seemed to understand the note of urgency in her voice. She nickered in response as Ana mounted then flew like the wind, surefooted hooves pounding against the rocky terrain of the mountain pass. The sun had moved in the sky by the time she reached the mountain's plateau, and one dizzying look down revealed the soldiers were no longer camped. They were on the move and marching in formation.

"Beast!" she cried out as Sterling charged onto the courtyard. "Beast!"

Her dragon didn't respond, although he usually heard her small voice and came to her at once.

Dismounting Sterling, she left the horse and rushed over the cracked palace steps. She threw open the doors and burst inside the foyer. Nothing. It was dark without a single candle flame burning. A cold wind whipped dried leaves down the hall against her face. The air smelled of old gunpowder smoke and mildew.

"Hora!" Ana called. "Beast!"

Neither answered. She found the vacant kitchen with an untended, cold oven. The dining room where she and Beast

VIVIENNE SAVAGE

had taken countless meals was dark, its hearth filled with ashes. Dust coated the long table and cobwebs clung to the chairs.

Nothing was as it should be. The room looked long abandoned, though she had eaten there only the previous morning.

Ana ran outside, frantic, and nearly stumbled over a broken cobblestone. The fountain was silent, no water flowing from its crown, the pool beneath empty and coated with moss. Trees that should have been full of golden and red leaves hung empty, their bare branches split.

"What's happening? Why is everything ruined? Beast! Beast!" She screamed his name into the air, but no returning cry came. Leaving Sterling to the decrepit courtyard, Ana raced around the side path and nearly skidded to her death on a wet patch where the secure wall had crumbled away. She backed up against the castle until the terror faded, her starved lungs gasping for air.

Dizziness gone, she picked her way carefully down the trail until she reached the gardens. No flowers bloomed, only thick grass and tall weeds.

The maze, the wind seemed to whisper to her.

Beast had never taken her to the maze, only Alistair in her dreams. Would the path be the same? Left, right, right. Left, right, right. She raced through the overgrown hedges, pushing through tangled branches that hadn't been trimmed or tended in years. Sharp spines on the leaves scratched her exposed skin, but she didn't slow.

When it seemed she was lost, Ana broke free of the wilderness into the center. The same statues stood on the corners, but unlike her dream, they were covered in moss. And there, curled around the pool, lay her motionless dragon instead of a handsome prince, his ember scales the dull, lifeless color of dirt. Her heart lurched.

"No…. No! Beast!"

She hurled herself across the distance and fell to her knees beside his great head, hands smoothing over his snout and neck.

"No, no, no. Please, you cannot leave me like this. You must awaken."

Tears dripped from her chin and splashed against the dragon's snout. Had he been ill all along? Had her recent dream of the prince been her subconscious thoughts telling her to look deeper. She hugged him and choked on the sobs rising in her throat. Dragons were supposed to be eternal.

"Princess?" his feeble voice whispered.

"Oh, my dragon, you frightened me."

"You were supposed to be far, far away. I didn't want you to see me this way, Ana. You must leave."

"No! The Dalborovian army is coming. They're at the base of the mountain."

"Let them come," he said. "I am lost, Princess. What you see is all that is left of my strength. I am defeated. Fading. You must go and save yourself."

❁ VIVIENNE SAVAGE

"What? No. How could I leave you when you're in danger? What sort of friend would I be?"

"A friend…."

"Yes, Beast. The dearest of friends, one worth throwing my life on the line between you and their army if I must. A friend beloved to me above all others. I hadn't realized how much until now, thinking I had lost you forever."

"It is too late for me."

"Please don't leave where I cannot follow. Don't go." She kissed his smooth snout where the scales weren't upraised or horned. "I love you too much, my silly dragon, to lose you now."

"My… Ana…." A final breath shuddered from Beast's lungs.

"No!" She grabbed at his face, fingers tugging on his great horns, half blind through her tears. Her heart shattered, and she threw her arms around him, great, heaving sobs shaking her body.

The air shimmered, a thousand colorful motes flickering outward from where they sat, expanding in a wave. Ana gasped. Her skin tingled as the palpable magic in the air filled and rushed through her. The air tasted sweet, smelling of roses and sunshine, and a chime rang upon the edge of her hearing, beautiful notes blended in perfect harmony.

A rainbow corona surrounded her dragon, as if he were glowing from within, each and every scale illuminated. She startled back, blinded by the light, and when it dimmed, her dragon was gone. A masculine figure lay in his place, bronzed from head to toe and adorned in garments she'd seen only in her dreams. White cloth was worn open to expose a muscular chest, and green tartan covered his developed legs.

Ana stumbled back with a hand raised to her mouth, staring at the body of her dream prince. His chest rose with a sharp inhale. Still surrounded by the golden shimmer of magic, he groaned and rolled onto his side. He pushed up onto his hands and knees.

"Alistair?" she whispered.

His eyes were smoldering amber, like fire dancing within alchemical spheres. Eyes that could drink her in and had held her attention for hours of casual conversation. Wavy red hair settled around his shoulders when the light dimmed, and fairy dust settled.

"I'm... alive?"

In his effort to rise, he staggered forward. Ana jumped up and caught him with both arms before he could collapse to the ground. He was so hard and warm against her, his body the perfect fit, no different than what she'd dreamed.

It wasn't a dream. It wasn't a dream at all. He's real. He's my dragon.

"Come, you should sit down."

"No, I only need a moment. I have not walked on two legs for thirteen years. It feels... it feels good to stand as a man again."

"I don't.... How is this...?" She shook her head,

  VIVIENNE SAVAGE

overwhelmed. As much as she wanted answers, more pressing matters required their focus. "Alistair, the army is on the march. They'll be here soon. We have hours at most."

"Then we must prepare. Do I still have your trust, my princess? Do you believe I will tell you everything in time?"

"Of course I do," she said without hesitation. She wanted answers now, but with an army closing in on them, she understood the delay.

Alistair shifted back into dragon form and lowered to his stomach for her to climb on, and then he took to the air. Sitting astride her dragon, they circled wide and high over the mountain.

Every inch of the mountaintop, from the lively grounds to the cold stone, had been restored to an immaculate state. Much like the castle's master, Benthwaite had come alive again. Below in the courtyard, castle guards and servants milled around in confusion.

"There, I see them," she called out. The army's line, organized two by two, stretched for miles, it seemed, hundreds of men in dark armor with glinting weapons marching up the mountain path. "They're closer than I thought."

"There are magic spells urging them along at an unnatural pace," Alistair said. "Can you not taste it on the wind?"

Returning to the castle grounds, Alistair landed and lowered for Ana to slide off. Then, in another blink, he shrunk down into his human guise.

"My lord!"

The arrival of the palace guard drew their attention. A dozen more giant men in armor followed behind the leader, and they towered over her, their shoulder-length hair windswept. They rippled with muscle beneath leather and chainmail.

"Captain Diarmad, my old friend." The two men clasped arms.

"What has happened? The last thing I recall with clarity was Eos—"

"There is no time for that now," Alistair broke in. "Dalborough has returned, and they've come in great numbers."

Diarmad's eyes widened. "My lord, we have no army, nor your mother's magic."

Alistair turned his gaze on Ana and extended his hand, which she took, stepping up beside him. "If the princess is willing, then we have all the magic we need. We must prepare for war."

Chapter 13

Alistair's strong hands squeezed her shoulders, grounding her back to reality. He was real. He had hands and fingers, bronzed skin no longer covered in red scales. And while it had been hours since the reawakening of the castle, every moment passed like a nebulous dream, a foggy consciousness that couldn't be true.

While Alistair commanded what soldiers they had, a group of young women rushed Anastasia into a chamber on the upper level and outfitted her in a set of war garments once worn by the Witch Queen herself. The robes consisted of tanned animal skins and dark silver silk spun from the fat, pony-sized onyx spiders of the lower forests. Almost impenetrable, they said while lacing her into it. The close fit startled Ana. She'd thought the Witch Queen had been a tall and slender woman of meager proportions.

Atop it, they'd given her another layer of fitted armor. The golden brown, molded leather cuirass was unforgiving to her ribs and bosom, compressing her breasts tighter than any corset.

Dressed for battle, Ana left the west wing and returned to the courtyard. Behind her, the castle doors shut and a loud thud from within indicated the entrance had been sealed. She took a deep breath and strode across the grass toward Alistair and a line of guardsmen. Compared to the approaching army, their forces seemed pitifully small, but every man and woman wore a determined expression on their face. The soldiers dispersed to their posts and Alistair turned to face her.

"You're certainly looking like a true warrior now. Like one of our own," Alistair said in a thoughtful voice. His thumb stroked one of the pauldrons covering her shoulder.

"I *am* one of you."

"That you are, lass."

Alistair cupped her chin and gazed into her eyes. "I've never fought a war. Taking on a group of adventurers who are no match for me is one thing, but to do this, I've got to have your help. I don't like asking this of you, and I'd rather send you into that damned castle to hide with the rest of my people, but…."

"I'm all you have."

He nodded. "And if I send you away to safety in the castle, they may overtake us and breach the defenses."

"Then the way I see it, I'm in danger no matter whether I'm hiding in the castle or here making a stand beside you." She set her hand against his chest, resting her palm above his heart. Unlike his soldiers, he wore no armor. She felt his hard muscles beneath her fingers and his powerful heartbeat thumping strong. "I'd rather fight. I've run away once, and that was enough."

Alistair kissed her. The press of his lips against her mouth struck Ana as both greedy and desperate, but she refused to think of it as a final kiss. She yielded to the claim he made with his tongue and mentally declared the ardent display as a promise of more.

When the prince stepped away, anticipation raised goose bumps on her skin, the crisp mountain air cooler but carrying the scent of their siege weapons and burning oil on the wind. His courage became infectious, coursing through her veins and urging her forward toward the cairn.

"I won't stray far, but if you need me, you scream, Ana. You hear me? You scream and I'll be here."

"I know."

The standing stones hummed with magic, and the air around them crackled with constrained energy. As she stepped within the circle, her skin tingled, every hair raising. There was no turning back, and while she'd never taken a life before Edward, she was prepared to defend her new home, no matter what it took.

From her vantage on the cliff, Ana saw the army making its way up the trail. Alistair's observation had been right, and foul magic blanketed the troops in an unnatural miasma. The oily presence coated her tongue, metallic and bitter. Rangvald must be with them, likely in the middle of the sinuous line where his spells would have an effective reach over most of the army.

War horns bellowed an ominous warning. The sound

echoed off the mountain peaks, and it took everything she had not to tremble on the spot.

No. She had to be strong and save lives using the talents sharpened by her months of devoted study. An entire castle of newly awakened servants counted on Ana's protection.

Counted on *both* of them.

Alistair ran toward the edge and dove forward, a smooth transition taking him from man to dragon in the blink of an eye. His clothes vanished, and sleek, ember red scales spread over his enormous body. He soared on his immense wings over the approaching army below and exhaled a wave of flames.

Time to help.

Taking her staff in both hands, Ana swung the weapon over her head in a slow arc. The cairn stones lit in a glorious blaze of green fire, runes etched into their surface flaring with ivory light.

She had to protect these people with as much ferocity as she'd protected herself from Edward.

The whole mountain responded to her summons. The ground quaked beneath the advancing troops and the rocks above them tumbled down the steep slopes. When the dust from the avalanche cleared, hundreds of soldiers lay crushed beneath boulders and dirt with more slipping to their doom down below. Seven siege weapons of the original dozen had survived the onslaught.

Ana searched the area for signs of the wizard Rangvald's survival, praying she'd knocked out their magical offensive

VIVIENNE SAVAGE

with her sneak attack.

She hadn't. Squinting, she located Rangvald below them on the uneven path with his staff raised, a crackling shell of energy surrounding him and the surviving soldiers. Pieces of rubble floated above them in the air then clattered down around the magical shield before reconstructing the missing section of the path, stone by stone and step by step.

Before she could cast her next spell, fire rained down from the sky, borne on dragon's breath.

For a moment, she admired Alistair's flight across the sky. His fiery breath blazed across the magical barrier, splintering the spell. Arrows zipped across the sky and forced her draconic prince to bank left, roaring in rage as he veered away from the mountain.

From there, everything happened at full speed. The army rushed up the road and spilled into the flat plateau beyond the courtyard.

Flaming projectiles soared across the sky. Ana called on the winds to steer them away from the castle. The first soared overhead and exploded harmlessly against the cliffs in the distance, but the second clipped the eastern tower. The stone bricks exploded. Green flames clung to the parapet, feeding off the oily fluid that dripped over the walls.

Catapults hurled a bounty of stone, the volley striking their castle at randomized points. Focusing, Anastasia found the threads of the ancient enchantment left by the Witch Queen herself and reinstated the castle's former protection spell. The Witch Queen had been a sorceress beyond her level of talent, an extraordinary woman who faced a much larger army.

It was too much for her.

She'd never pull it off, the spell too old, neglected for too long.

As doubts crept into her thoughts, she remembered the dozens of maids, castle staff, and the soldiers fighting for their lives. More than her own life was at stake. They were all counting on her, each and every one.

Especially her dragon.

With her faith renewed in herself, she whirled toward the castle and tilted her staff toward the structures under assault, holding it in her right hand. Grasping those magical fibers with her mind, Ana held on with all that she had until agony clawed behind her eyes and lights pulsed at the edges of her vision.

She couldn't let go. No matter what, she couldn't release the spell. She poured all that she had into the incantation until the barrier snapped in place, the sheer effort of commanding so much power winding her. She gasped for air as sweat beaded upon her brow and stung her eyes.

Alistair took out two trebuchets in one pass, sweeping them up with his claws and smashing them against the cliffs. An arrow larger than anything Ana had ever seen flew through the air.

A dragon lance. Something rumored to exist only in

fables and war stories of the past.

"Alistair!"

He twisted in the air, graceful and sleek, but not fast enough to miss the projectile completely. The spear sliced across his chest.

The sounds of battle echoed across the mountain. Men yelling, swords clashing, and the explosive boom of rock smashing against stone.

From her vantage, Ana tried to aid the battle where she could. With the cairn and staff boosting her power, she swirled the winds to buffet away arrows, raised shields around her soldiers, and called lightning bolts down from the sky to decimate their enemy.

Little by little, the Benthwaite guard pushed their attackers back.

The sky lit up and a resounding boom threatened to force Ana to her knees in pain. The entire mountain shook from the might of Rangvald's magic. She stumbled to the side and thrust the end of the staff into the ground, regaining her balance in time to prepare for his next assault.

He forced the winds against her, hurled acidic bolts, and did everything in his power to occupy her attention. While she was focused on him, she couldn't help the soldiers, and the enemy pressed their advantage, swarming over the grounds.

While she was distracted with defending the castle, Rangvald decided to play dirty. A streak of energy hurtled toward Anastasia, but Alistair's huge body became her shield.

The destructive spell collided against the dragon's chest and erupted in sparks, searing through his scales.

"Alistair!" she screamed, panicked.

He plummeted from the skies, his death spiral making Ana's heart leap into her throat.

No. He couldn't be dead. Please no, she pleaded.

Suddenly, his wings snapped out, and Alistair coasted over the enemy line, directly toward their wizard. The arcane attacks ended with a single snap of his jaws. He crushed the unprepared wizard between his teeth, bringing an end to Rangvald's terror. Ana's reprieve was short lived.

The Dalborovian army flooded the castle grounds, an endless wave of black armored soldiers with terrible war machines. A dozen men turned and made their way up the winding path toward her, but she'd prepared magical traps before their arrival. Thorned vines whipped out and dragged the first two men over the cliff, while great bouts of blue fire forced others back. Ana directed a concussive blast down the steppe and knocked the remaining soldiers back, head over asses.

Or so she thought.

A twig snapped to her left, off the pathway, and Anastasia whirled toward the approaching knight in full armor, a helmet obscuring her view of his face. He held a shield in one hand and a sword in the other, the former polished to a mirror shine and buzzing with magical energy. Somehow, he'd run the gauntlet of her spells, the lone survivor of the many Dalborovian soldiers who rushed for the mountain. Alistair continued to pick them off from below. From the corner of her eye, she saw him descend toward a siege weapon.

"Step closer and I will kill you. I won't miss at this distance," she promised. The staff hummed with restrained power, but her mind was tired, her physical body equally exhausted and on the brink of collapse. She couldn't maintain it forever. The battle of magic with Rangvald had pushed her to the limits of her ability.

"Anastasia?"

The voice echoing from within the metal helmet made her pause. Then her heart was racing fast and hard in her chest, coiling inky tendrils of nausea throughout her gut. No. He couldn't be alive. She'd stabbed him enough times and left him for dead.

"Edward?"

He removed the helmet and tossed it aside to stare at her. He looked hale and hearty, a flush of health on his cheeks, rosy from the exertion of overtaking the mountain. Sweat slicked his dark curls against his brow, but his blue eyes shone with fury.

The staff nearly dropped from Anastasia's hands.

Her former betrothed lurched forward a step. "Surprised to see me after you left me for dead?"

"You tried to rape me!" Recovering her wits, she raised the staff again. They were close. Too close. One stride of his long legs covered too much ground.

"You ought to have submitted like a proper wife. Now I find you here leading these barbarians. You could have been a queen!" He swept an armored hand at her and sneered in disgust. "What is that ridiculous outfit?"

"I wear the battle robes of the Queen of Ocland. Better to die with them than to live as your sex slave."

He moved, but an excess of spellcasting had retarded her reflexes, making her feel sluggish and slow. With power sizzling at her fingertips, she hurled a fireball at him with her free hand, but he batted it away, the spell a mere annoyance. A split second later, Edward's gauntlet collided with her cheek. Pain exploded across her cheekbone. She flew backward, struck off balance by the powerful blow, and crumpled in the grass.

"We came to save you from this beast, and you have the foolish audacity to side with it?"

The world spun. She tasted blood in her mouth, the sharp tang of it on her tongue. "He isn't a beast! He's more of a man than you will ever be."

Using the staff, she returned to her feet and shook off the dizziness. Before Edward could strike her again, she lashed out with a buffeting strike, channeling wind and sheer force into a solid blast meant to knock him away. Edward barely swayed.

Spells slid off of his shield like water over oiled cloth. Her eyes darted to the left and saw Alistair dodging another dragon lance. He barrel rolled through the air, twirling in a feat of acrobatics she hadn't thought dragons flexible enough

VIVIENNE SAVAGE

to perform, then swooped down and dragged another cannon off the ledge with his hind claws.

"Your father promised you to me," Edward taunted. "It's no wonder you've turned savage when your own family no longer wants you."

She ignored him, refusing to fall prey to his mind games. Every magical attack she tried bounced off of him, but they kept him at bay.

"If you won't be mine, then no one will have you."

Edward penned her in, the higher ridge of the mountain to one side and open space to the other. His combat experience and shield combined into an impenetrable forward defense. She struggled to split it with her magic and screamed as his sword whistled toward her.

He was going to cut her down, and Alistair wouldn't arrive in time to save her.

Despite the likelihood of her demise, Anastasia didn't give in. She clung to her consciousness, tenacious will forcing her tiring arms to endure. She raised the staff once more and deflected his strike.

Then she summoned everything she had and placed it in one spell. All of her emotion—despair and hope, anger at Edward, and love for Alistair—unbottled at once. Lightning fell from the sky, raining from the heavens in multiple shades of color.

Fairy lights. A spell only the descendants of the fairies could accomplish. And somehow, she'd pulled it off at the moment when her life hung in the balance.

A sizzling, mauve bolt struck Edward. It tossed him to the ground, seared him, then lightning struck twice more, serene cobalt blue and teal green. A branching network of burns discolored Edward's face and disappeared beneath the neck of his chest piece.

Alistair landed and rushed forward on four legs with murder in his eyes, only to draw up short when he saw Edward's motionless body stretched over the ground.

Chapter 14

SOBBING, ANASTASIA LAUNCHED herself into Alistair's arms, colliding with his scaled chest. His arms raised automatically to embrace the tiny woman, and the flat heel of his clawed hand pressed between her shoulders. "We did it. We defeated them!"

What remained of Dalborough's forces had turned tail and run without their leaders to command them.

"We did, my princess. That we did."

"Are you all right? Were you hurt? You were amazing, soaring into the battle as you did. Let me look at you." Her hands began to move over his massive chest, fingers traversing his scales once she pulled back to inspect him for injury. He'd lost a few, creating sore spots that burned beneath her touch.

Alistair laughed through the pain, and for her benefit, he nuzzled her cheek with his snout. "I am fine, Ana, truly. See?"

"Look at me, babbling out a million questions when you must have so much you need to do. And the rest of your people, they must be so bewildered. We must see to them, and to you."

Taking his human shape felt odd. After so many years in dragon form, he had forgotten what it was like to stand on two legs. His dreams hadn't prepared him for the reality. Everything ached, and yet it was worth it to have her in his arms.

Hugging her close hurt so good, despite bruises and a number of cuts under his tattered clothes, each one stinging beneath a layer of sweat. "Yes. I must see to them. You're right," he agreed.

Alistair leaned back on unsteady feet and raised his head to look at a number of people awaiting his command. Dozens of archers stood on the castle battlements, soldiers with swords and wooden shields on standby observing them in silence.

"There will be plenty of time to talk." Ana moved to his side and took his hand. "We should secure the castle and see that everyone is fed and tended. The army is gone for now, and it will be weeks before they can mount another attack. *If* they even try."

Anastasia took charge without awaiting his command. The timid princess of months ago no longer existed, and in her place stood a formidable warrior queen. Suddenly, the dragon prince realized he wasn't the only one to change. She had grown into a capable woman worthy of the throne beside him. His pride for her surged, second only to the love swelling in his heart.

"Aye. A good idea," he agreed. Pride wouldn't allow him to limp beside her. He gritted through the pain and moved tall at her side. As they approached, the many men and women lowered to a knee to greet them.

VIVIENNE SAVAGE

"Your Majesty," they greeted him.

For them, the thirteen years had been no more than a day. He'd have much to share with them. Many explanations, but in the meantime, he had only orders. "Have the uninjured assemble in the audience chamber at once. I want the five men most able to stand to remain on the tower watch. I will address them personally after the wounded are accounted for."

"Of course, my king." Diarmad put a hand to his chest and bowed. Then he took off to relay the order to his guardsmen.

The corridors teemed with flesh and blood people who had awakened in time to see a war. Alistair and Ana made their way inside toward the audience chamber, no longer a gallery of statues, now filled with living, breathing people.

"They were the statues," she whispered in awe.

"Aye, lass," Alistair confirmed, a heavy sadness in his voice. "I condemned not only myself, but every living being here. They lost thirteen years of their lives because of me."

The servants and maids of the castle who had defended it during the siege watched them move with wide eyes. Two young women hurried to them with woven baskets filled with bandages and bottles of healing salve.

"My king, you're injured!"

"Thank you, Adaira, but care for Princess Anastasia first," he said. "I can see to myself."

"I am fine," Ana assured the maids. "Please, if you'll help me, we can see to our wounded soldiers first."

Humbled once more by her selflessness, Alistair watched

as Ana took charge of the menders. She did more than delegate orders; she helped nurse the injured with her own hands, no matter how small or great the wound, while he saw to his remaining guardsmen.

Most of the warriors were much like their king, refusing to acknowledge their wounds. Along the way, Alistair gave orders to secure the mountain, for their archers to remain alert, and for any able-bodied members of the castle staff to join them.

And then he told the remaining members of his loyal staff everything.

"Though many of you are too unwell to stand here now, I owe you all my eternal gratitude—and my apologies," he began.

He didn't take his father's throne. It didn't feel right. They'd been attacked for the second time because of him after all, and they'd all lost countless time with their loved ones who didn't live within the castle. He closed his eyes and sighed.

"It may seem like only a day to you, but thirteen years have passed. All of you, including me, have been under a fairy's curse. And the fault is mine. I brought this upon us all."

He held nothing back, enduring shouts of dismay and justified anger. Tears. And finally forgiveness. They had all shared his pain, and when it was over, he dismissed them for the evening to rest and recover.

"Come, that means you as well." Ana stepped up from behind him and took him by the arm. "You'll be of no use to anyone if you collapse from exhaustion."

"But—"

"Please," she whispered, "for me."

She guided him to the large bathing room with her arm around his shoulders and crouched beside the brass fixtures and unfamiliar knobs. Eos had transformed his castle into a place filled with strange new conveniences. The enchantments spun for Ana's benefit remained, and he wondered if it was the fairy's way of granting them a gift.

Seconds later, steam billowed up and around them, accompanied by the smell of fresh water in the air.

"You will not leave?" Alistair asked when she emerged, drying her wet fingers against her robes.

"Your room?"

"The castle."

Ana shook her head and smiled. "No. This is my home, Alistair." She kissed his cheek and guided him to the door. "Meet me in the library once you've freshened."

Alistair tried to smile in return. "To ask me more questions?"

"Of course."

He yearned for a bath, and realization of the many things he could do once again flooded back to him at once. Read a book, sit at a table, soak in a tub. Embrace a woman. Without warning, he surrounded Ana with both of his arms and squeezed her tight, burying his face in her hair. How did she still smell so good even after a battle, with the scent of blood and smoke on her skin?

"I'll meet you in an hour," he promised, sending her off with a soft pat on her bottom.

With so much blood and grime clinging to his skin, he rinsed the filth away first with a bucket of water while standing over the grate to the castle cistern. Then he soaked in the deep basin until a concerned maid rapped on the door. By the time he retired to his bedroom, his joints protested movement, and his muscles screamed for rest. But he couldn't sleep yet. Not until he'd taken Ana in his arms one more time and spoken his heart.

Hora floated in the center of the room, wispy and translucent without the thin guise of humanity granted by magic. She turned to face him and smiled.

"Hora." He turned and gazed at the woman who had been his governess since infancy. "You're still here."

"Eos has given me this time to say farewell to you."

By habit, he stepped forward to embrace her, only to remember at the last second that he could not. Spirits, even those as strong as Hora, had no substance. She smiled at him and lifted a hand to his cheek. Alistair felt only cool air.

"Your mother and father would be proud of you this day, Alistair. So proud. Not only did you guard this castle, but you owned up to your own shortcomings. You admitted your wrong."

"I don't deserve their forgiveness."

"You do. War is ugly. It is cruel. Wars have started over

lesser crimes and smaller slights than the loss of a family, Alistair." She dropped her hand and stepped back. "Let the cycle of vengeance end with today's battle."

"I promise."

"Good. Know that I am proud of you as well, Alistair. Anastasia is a good match for you. Treasure her always."

"I will, Hora. I swear it on my scales."

Hora smiled. "So much like your father you are." Seconds later, she faded away, leaving Alistair alone with his room and the fading sunlight.

For the sake of Ana's modesty, as well as concealing wounds that hadn't yet healed, he donned a tunic with the family's green tartan. For once, he didn't mind the cold, unyielding floor beneath him as he adjusted the garment in place.

Alistair didn't shave, too eager to see her again to delay their reunion any longer, and with damp hair around his shoulders, he pushed through his exhaustion to pound down the hallways—lively corridors filled with conversation and household staff. Family members without blood ties.

Despite the men lost on the battlefield, a celebration carried on inside their grand dining hall. He only slowed to accept tearful hugs from overjoyed castle residents, the library his true destination. Warmth from the hearth greeted him as he stepped inside to join his chosen bride. Ana had beaten him, curled up in her favorite chair with a cup of tea in her favorite night rail and dressing gown. A second cup sat beside the teapot.

"I wasn't sure if you even liked tea, let alone how you prefer it," Ana said by way of greeting. She smiled shyly at him.

"I do. With sugar. Too much, as Hora would say, but I favor sweets." He took a seat in the chair across from her.

Her smile wavered. "She said goodbye to me moments ago. She's truly gone for good now."

"Aye, lass. She passed away a year before the castle fell, quietly in her sleep. I'm not sure why she was brought back during the curse, but I was grateful for her presence and the company she gave during the dark times of these past thirteen years."

Ana quieted while pouring his tea. She added three heaping teaspoons of sugar before passing him the fragile cup. "A curse…."

Anxiety gnawed an acidic hole into the pit of his stomach, and he directed his gaze to the surface of his tea to avoid making eye contact. "Yes. A curse laid upon me by my fairy godmother."

"What fairy would do such a thing?"

"Her name is Eos, though that's only short. She's known to my people as Eleanor of the Southern Wind."

She blinked. "Eos?"

"You know the name?"

"Though I've never met her, my mother's mother went by that name. As far as I know, she's never been a part of my life. Like all fairies, she gave her child to her human lover and visited her infrequently. But why did she curse you?"

He had been waiting for the question, fearing it, but knowing he owed her the truth. "After Dalborough attacked my home and killed my family, I sank into despair. Over time, I let rage consume me, and it became my only motivation to live. I burned villages and pillaged towns. I hurt many people, killed others, and I did it all thinking I deserved justice."

"Oh, Alistair," she whispered, hands lifted to her lips and tears shining in her eyes.

"All I did was bring pain and misery, Ana. I had truly become a beast, and so Eos cursed me to live as one until I could find someone who truly loved me.

"Me."

Alistair set the teacup aside and lowered to his knees in front of her. He claimed one of her hands, warmed by the mug, and pressed his cheek to her palm. "You reminded me of what it was like to care about another person's well-being, lass. You *saved* me."

"But…." Her cheeks flushed hot. "You must think the most wicked, horrible things about me. I threw myself at you in those dreams," she whispered. "I was brazen."

Her words brought a surge of heat to his loins, awakened by the memory of their kiss in the spring and the slick sensation of her naked skin to his skin. He'd thought her to be no different from any woman of his kingdom, full of confidence and a desire to take what she wanted, with sexual needs she planned to fulfill.

"How could I think anything wicked when you came to this castle and gave me a reason to live again?" For over twelve years, he had endured a half-life of loneliness in the shadows, the days in her company the only ones filled with light.

"I was very... forward."

"Discovering those dreams were connected was as much a surprise to me as it was to you." Her touch felt so good, better than the warmth of a campfire on a frigid night. He turned his head and kissed each fingertip before whispering, "But I looked forward to them whenever they came."

"That's reassuring."

"I would never do anything to hurt you. I am still your dragon, Ana. Yours."

"I still can't believe this is all real. That you really can turn from a dragon to a man."

"Aye," Alistair said. "Many of us in Ocland have this gift, a secret rarely, if ever, shared with outsiders."

"You mean, there are more dragons out there who can become human? Or are you humans who become dragons? Which is your natural shape?"

Alistair blinked at her. "My natural shape? I... I don't think I know anymore," he admitted. "No one does."

"It doesn't matter then. You're still my dragon."

The Anastasia he'd come to know would have a million and one questions, her inquisitive nature spitting out one inquiry after the next. Exhaustion rendered his princess unusually silent.

VIVIENNE SAVAGE

"The hour has grown late. Come, I'll escort you to your room."

Hand in hand, they traveled through the castle to her old bedroom, where he kissed her at the door with all of his passion and desire. Ana sighed sweetly as they parted, eyes half-lidded and a dreamy smile on her face.

Leaving her was an exercise in willpower. Thanks to her, there would be time on the morrow for an in-depth discussion of their futures. Tomorrow, he would claim her as his in every way.

Chapter 15

TENDER FINGERS AND an even gentler voice disturbed Ana's sleep. She awakened to a nervous chambermaid lurking beside her bed. "Princess Anastasia?"

The young woman's name swam into her memories, recalled once she'd blinked the sleep from her eyes. "What is it Fiona?" She'd met Fiona, among a handful of the other maids, when the group outfitted her in the Witch Queen's battle robes.

"King Alistair has asked that I attend you until such a time that you demand my presence no longer."

"Oh! I haven't had a lady's maid in months. I shouldn't need one at—"

The girl carried on, voice strong and determined as she said, "But it would please me greatly, Princess, to be in your service. You who have saved us all from sleep and our beloved king from death. Please allow me to guide you through life in our castle. I beg you…."

"I…." Touched by the girl's open display of honesty, she tilted her head in a wordless nod.

Fiona washed Ana's hair and helped brush the knots from it. For the first time in months, the princess donned multiple layers of attire. It smelled of fresh lavender and roses, the fabric soft as flower petals. The simple cream, floor-length underdress kissed her skin like silk, worn beneath an overdress in copper-gold, its matching bodice in the Oclander style. She'd never shown so much cleavage in all of her life, and flushed as she tried to adjust the neckline of the underdress to conceal more bosom.

"His Highness requested that you join him for breakfast in his study, if you so wish, else I am to bring you whatever you like."

"No, that won't be necessary. I'll join him."

Alistair's personal study adjoined his bedchamber and was one of the few rooms she hadn't explored during her time in the castle. Fiona left her at the door with a smile and a wink.

The prince—no, the king, rose from his seat the moment she entered.

Her cheeks flushed hot, the memory of their shared kisses and encounter in the hot spring sending a jolt straight to her core. She'd thrown herself at her dream prince, and for a few minutes, she'd had him at her mercy, his flesh hot, alive, and stiff beneath her fingers.

"My princess," he breathed.

Alistair crossed to her in three steps, closing the distance and seizing her mouth. He kissed her with energy and passion, the spark between them sizzling within moments.

And it was so much better than her dreams. So much better than the kiss of the previous night when he'd been restrained and careful. He held back nothing this time, without inhibitions or caution, claiming her with white-hot lust that sent sparks curling through her core, sizzling out to every nerve ending.

She sighed when it ended, only to draw back and glide her palms over his chest. He wore his tunic parted again. Sliding her hands beneath it and over his chest, she searched for visible wounds and injuries. None. He'd healed overnight.

Her eyes raised to his smug face.

"I told you I would be fine."

"It's remarkable."

"We heal incredibly fast."

"Dragons or Oclanders in general?" She smoothed her hand over his bronzed flesh, mesmerized by the hard muscle.

"Not all Oclanders have this gift, lass. Many of us do—men and women both—but it doesn't make us invincible. We're only tougher to kill. Especially dragons."

"Are you the last?" She tilted her gaze up to his and searched his face.

"I may be. If there are more who survived the war, we haven't crossed paths."

"But what about before the war? Did you know any others?"

"My father's sister lost her life in the first attack."

Guilt washed through her. "I'm sorry. I didn't mean to dredge up the past."

Alistair shook his head and stroked his hand up her back. "One day soon, I promise, I will tell you everything about my

VIVIENNE SAVAGE

people. I want you to know, especially if…."

"If what?"

He gazed down at her, eyes gleaming with intensity. "Would you remain here beside me, Anastasia? As my queen?"

Her chest tightened, too small to contain her swelling heart. "Do you really mean it?"

"Of course I mean it. I…" He leaned down and kissed her, short and sweet. "…I love you, and I pray you can love a beast such as me in return for each day of the rest of our lives."

"Silly dragon, you aren't a beast," she whispered as she lifted to her toes to kiss him again. She savored the moment, pressing in close and twining her arms around his neck. "You're *my* dragon, and I couldn't love anyone more."

He turned his face and skimmed his nose against her cheek, then spoke against her ear in a husky murmur. "Are you hungry?"

"Not for breakfast."

"Good."

He lifted her as if she weighed no more than a feather and carried her to his room next door, kicking the door shut behind them. After he set her on her feet again, Ana turned and presented her back to him.

"Help me?" she asked. She dragged her thick mass of hair over one shoulder, revealing the tight lacings of her dress and corset.

"Are you so eager to strip?" he teased.

"Please," she begged.

With a skilled hand and a few movements, Alistair unlaced her dress. A couple tugs loosened the snug embrace it formed around her midsection and ribs, and once it fell away, he removed the rest of her outer garments. At the end, she stood in only a pristine, ivory chemise, trembling with desire and anticipation.

"May I?" Alistair whispered against her ear from behind. She nodded.

"I didn't hear you, sweet princess. What am I to do next?"

"Undress me," she whispered. "Please."

"No." He snaked an arm around her waist and squeezed one breast, teasing the taut tip through her undergarment. "You are to be a queen, Anastasia. You beg no one for anything."

"Not even you?"

"Not even me. You are to be my equal in every way, my love."

"Then undress me, my king. Make love to me. Make me yours as I surely plan to make you mine."

"As you command."

Then the chemise was gone, the tie unfastened that allowed it to glide loosely down her body and pool around her ankles, removing the last scrap of modesty between her and his hands. That morning, when Fiona dressed her, she'd discovered women of Ocland didn't wear pantalets.

She was bare. Stripped. A chill danced across her skin, raising goose bumps down her arms and hardening her exposed nipples. Both of his strong hands fit around her waist easily, then he scooped a breast with each palm and squeezed Ana back against him.

Alistair adjusted his stance and nudged forward with his pelvis. The ideal position wedged his stiff bulge between her cheeks, provoking a startled noise from Anastasia. She melted against him, surrendering to her own curiosity while wishing he was also absent of clothes.

"Here I am, the shy virgin of the storybooks I've read so often," she confessed in a whisper. "In the books, it's always perfect. The girls always know what to do."

"Have you any doubts about what is to happen next?" Alistair teased her. He ran a circle over her bare hip, finding a ticklish spot. She squirmed. "Your behavior in our dream led me to believe otherwise."

Heat flashed over her cheeks. "As I said, I know what happens next, but something tells me it isn't like the… books."

"It isn't." Alistair's lips lowered to her throat and closed for a playful nip. Wherever his fingers drifted over her body, electricity jumped between them. "The real thing is nothing like the books in my library. Nothing like anything you've ever read. It will be superior to any act you'll find in any book. In every way."

The breath whistled in and out of her lungs. Her emotions found an odd balance between terror and yearning, her need for Alistair unsated by dreams of kissing and mere touches.

When he growled, the noise vibrated through his chest and reached her ears as a throaty rumble. Even in his human body, the dragon remained a powerful part of his personality. It was him. He was it. And while she'd set him free from the curse's trap, the animal continued to lurk beneath the surface.

Would he take her like an animal? Would he bend her over the mattress on her hands and knees, claiming her like a beast in heat? The idea of it clenched her insides, sending a bolt of electricity directly to her core.

According to her mother, a true bride of Creag Morden lost her virginity on her wedding night.

But she wasn't her mother, and as far as she was concerned, she was no longer the princess of Creag Morden.

She was Ana, chosen Queen of King Alistair, a man more kind and deserving of her affection than any crown prince from the west.

"Kiss me again?"

"Gladly."

Ana twisted around in his embrace and raised both arms to circle around the dragon shifter's neck. She gazed into eyes as warm as toffee, flecked with hints of green through their golden brown irises.

"You're beautiful," he said as he dipped his head down for another kiss. His lips trailed from her mouth down her throat. "Magnificent."

Lower and lower he traveled, until his mouth skimmed the slope of her breast. His lips teased tender, sensitive flesh, but never drifted to her rosy, pink nipples. The seductive taunt only made her want him more. Then he pulled away.

"Alistair? What are you doing?"

His low chuckle puffed warm air across her dampened skin, but he gave no answer. Instead, he took a single step back from her.

"Do you plan to keep me in suspense?"

"Have you never watched a man remove his clothing?"

Anastasia bit her lower lip. She'd seen nothing of even Edward that night.

"Almost," she whispered. "But it wasn't pleasant."

Alistair paused with his fingers on the buttons of his shirt. The questioning in his face and hesitation, mixed with concern, was all she needed to see to know she'd made the right choice.

"But watching you isn't unpleasant. Don't make me wait. I'm cold," she added with a hint of teasing in her voice.

"Get on the bed, Ana."

"Are you going to join me?"

A slow smile spread across his face, wicked and sinful, and completely breathtaking. "Aye, lass. But I want to see you there first."

The silk-lined, feather down blanket cradled her as she lowered to the bed. It was cool against her bare skin, and his scent clung to the soft material. Lying before him naked and wanting, she felt a strange sense of vulnerability. Her nipples tightened, imploring her to run her fingers over a taut peak in a poor attempt to alleviate the stiffness.

Alistair groaned. The remaining two buttons popped and

Beauty & the Beast

scattered over the floor. When he unfastened the strap to his kilt, he let the garment fall. Licking her lips, Ana leaned up on her elbows to watch. Until their shared dream at the maze, she'd always wondered what the men of Ocland wore beneath their kilts.

Nothing. Like their female counterparts, they wore absolutely nothing. Without his clothing, the sight of sheer, masculine perfection greeted Ana, chiseled pectorals and a strong torso above his washboard abdomen.

He joined her on the bed, moving beside her on his knees, hiding nothing from her view. Ana leaned forward, shy at first, but increasing confidence led her index finger down a golden-red trail. The soft hairs led to the erect rod jutting from his pelvis. It flexed a little higher, angled toward his navel.

"May I…?"

"It's yours to do with as you please."

Hers. A tiny shiver tingled over Ana's body. Touching Alistair's manhood was like touching silk, the flesh smooth beneath her inquisitive fingers but firm as living steel. Even better was the way his breath hitched and his pelvis thrust forward when her slim digits curled around him.

"In our dream, I had so many wicked thoughts," she confessed.

"And now?"

"I still have them, but I suppose I'm a little afraid."

"You never have to fear anything from me, Ana. Do you trust me?"

VIVIENNE SAVAGE

"Yes."

"Then let me show you how little the books compare."

After taking her hand from his cock, Alistair lavished each of her fingertips with a kiss. The stubble at his jaw scraped against her palm and down her wrist, his kisses reaching the sensitive skin of her inner forearm. With only the slightest of nudges, he encouraged her to lie back fully against the blanket.

The path of kisses continued down her side, over her ribs and against her hip. He caressed his hands down her legs until she relaxed, and then he shifted his body between them.

"My lovely Ana." He pressed a kiss to her navel. "My brave, selfless princess." His mouth trailed to her lower tummy. "My fierce sorceress queen."

Her whole body tensed, thrumming with anticipation and longing. Every light kiss tortured and tested her already fragile composure.

"Your smell…" As Alistair breathed her in, the tip of his nose skimmed the crease of her inner thigh. "…it's intoxicating."

The air in her lungs became insufficient, hummingbird breaths failing to quench her thirst for oxygen. Her pulse sped faster, her lust soaring higher, and then her dragon's tongue divided the wet slit at his mercy. Her legs trembled.

"H-how many times have you done this?" she asked, voice quivering as much as her body.

Alistair leaned on his elbows to gaze at her. "You're the only time that matters."

The sentiment, whether true or not, warmed Ana down to her toes. Her belly tightened with anticipation, relieved only by the strong fingers guiding her legs to part. Seconds later, when he touched her wet center, she melted into the sheets and closed her eyes.

"We've barely started yet, lass. There's much more to do."

Anastasia opened her legs to him fully, baring herself and feeling even more brazen as she did. His fingers glided over slick moisture then teased the tender, sensitive button at the apex of her folds. From that moment, nothing else mattered. Her hips jerked upward, following his touch when it withdrew. His fingers circled and teased, testing her wetness and the tight cling of her body with the occasional stroke. His fingers sank in with ease, then they were gone again.

"I don't think I can bear much more, Alistair. I... I need to feel you. I need to have you inside me. I want to be yours," Anastasia hissed between her teeth, on the precipice between torture and sweet release.

"Not yet, my love."

"I need it. I want... I want..." Her words were lost to moans as he glided the throbbing length between glistening folds, giving only a taste of what she desired. "...you to be mine," she finished on a pant.

Her dragon paused, becoming statue still and just as silent. For a brief moment, Ana panicked beneath him and wondered if she'd ruined the mood and tarnished the intimacy between them with her claim.

VIVIENNE SAVAGE

"Yours," Alistair whispered. Without another word, he kissed her hard, dominating her mouth with the tip of his tongue. The taste of her own arousal flavoring it, an inexplicable turn-on, everything about him making her writhe with unrestrained lust.

Then he was entering her in excruciatingly slow increments, granting all of the time needed for her body to grow accustomed to his girth. After another inch, her lover's body tensed. Every defined muscle grew taut and his breaths quickened.

"Alistair?" She touched her fingers to his cheek. "What's wrong?"

After a quiet groan, his lips ghosted over her temple. "You're so tight, Ana. That's all. Am I hurting you?"

"No."

He bucked forward, claiming her with another inch. Ana's eyes rolled back, and she shuddered beneath him, but her impulsive nature won out and forced her to take control of the situation. He was too slow. Too slow, and she needed much more of him.

Raising both legs from the bed, Ana planted her heels above his firm buttocks and dragged him down to meet her with one sharp tug. A fleeting bite of discomfort bloomed in her core as they joined in a snug embrace.

"Ana?"

"I'm okay," she grunted out, wishing her voice sounded sensual and alluring. It was more of a croak than anything.

He remained motionless above her until her breaths evened and her body relaxed, and then he withdrew without warning and thrust home a second time. Ana cried out in startled pleasure, gripping his shoulders tight.

"Again."

Her dragon obliged with tireless strokes. She lost herself to the rhythm of their primitive dance, guided by his strong hands and sensual murmurs. Pleasure coiled within her and became a tightly wound spring ready to snap. She didn't know where to grab him or where to hold, so she settled for touching him everywhere. Her fingers skimmed from his shoulders down to his arms, caressing thick biceps she'd admired. She stroked his back, nails biting the rippling muscle beneath her hands whenever he reached a particularly delicious depth.

When she arched beneath him, his head dipped low. He sought her breasts with his lips, skimming the sensitive tips and nibbling each between his teeth. His mouth sealed around one tender peak and sucked. She clenched around him, and he mirrored her ecstasy with an approving grunt.

As every panted sigh came quicker, her cries rose until Alistair shifted above her and united them at the perfect, splendid angle. One triumphant moment of bliss rippled through her core and the tension shattered, delivering her to ecstasy that consumed her like a million sparks igniting throughout her body.

Alistair groaned out her name and stiffened. For a single, glorious moment, Ana experienced the transcendent joy of being one with the man above her. His every thought and emotion were open to her, as if they shared one body, one heart, and one mind.

They collapsed together in a limp pile, chests heaving. Alistair wrapped his arms around her and rolled to his back while cradling her close to his side. Ana pressed her cheek into his shoulder and waited for her breaths to even. Her heart slammed an unrelenting tempo against her ribs, the air huffing in and out of her thirsty lungs.

Even her dragon had worked himself up into a sweat. His brows, shoulders, and chest shone, moisture glistening over the flawless abs she had wanted to kiss. "Are you all right?"

"Mm, more than all right," she replied. She peeked up at his sated grin and smiled too.

"Better than your books?"

"Much better." Her books hadn't come close to describing how it felt, pale comparisons to the reality.

"We are mated for life, Anastasia. You are my queen from this day forward. We have no formal ceremonies, only the sacred vows we whisper to one another."

Her head raised from the pillow. "What?"

"I chose to share part of my dragon soul with you." His fingers smoothed over her silky, untamed waves. Her wide, owlish eyes continued to stare into him as comprehension flooded her mind.

"Aren't dragons eternal, Alistair?"

"As are their mates. Now you know the secret to the Witch

Queen's long life," he whispered. He hesitated while watching her, losing the confidence that fueled his decision to claim her physically and spiritually. "Have I behaved out of turn? Have I upset you?"

"I…." Ana shook her head, and her stormy eyes misted over with moisture. His hand raised to her cheek before the first tears began to fall, and then he wiped them away.

"You are crying. Ana, please. Tell me your thoughts. Tell me if I've upset you."

"I'm not upset, silly. I'm crying because I'm happy. Because I can't believe it's true. None of this seems real anymore." She inhaled a few shaky breaths, only to surrender to impulse and throw her arms around his neck. They hugged tight, laughing together, her giggles and his warm chuckles the only noise in the bedroom.

"I love you with all of my being, with all that I am."

VIVIENNE SAVAGE

Epilogue

ALISTAIR PRONOUNCED ANASTASIA as his queen before all members of his court able to attend the grand festival that evening, and from that day forward, she slept beside him in their royal bedchamber. During their days, they made plans to rebuild the kingdom and restore Cairn Ocland to its former glory. And during the nights, her eager husband made up for his thirteen years of forced celibacy.

With each passing day, he reaffirmed their love with small tokens of affection. Although they weren't always physical gifts, she reveled in experiencing a tender side of her new husband. She taught him to enjoy tea in the garden, where the reawakened servants brought them delicious brunches and midday meals. He led her on small adventures to different parts of the castle and their grounds, sometimes trekking down the mountain to find the flowers growing among the rocky crags covered in green.

At night, he joined her in the observatory, his arms around her waist while she searched the skies and discovered new stars.

Their lives were happy, and she couldn't ask for anything more.

Except the chance to visit home.

"Something's been weighing on your mind. What is it?" he asked during an evening stroll, days after their triumph over Dalborough.

"I need to go home, Alistair."

"Home?" A wrinkle creased between his brows. "To take the flower to your mother."

"Yes, but I need to face my father and speak to him. I need to tell him... so many things. Maybe he doesn't deserve to know what's happened, but he's my father. I love him."

Alistair slid his arms around her and set his chin on her shoulder. "You are a very wise woman, my queen."

"Would you come with me?"

"Your father may take offense to you arriving on the back of a dragon," he mused thoughtfully. His fingers ran down her spine, tracing the laces she couldn't wait for him to loosen in their bedroom.

"My father wouldn't dare challenge or harm you now that you're mine. If he doesn't like it, then..." She swallowed and leaned back to search his face, reminded of how she'd felt the moment she learned her dragon and her prince were one and the same. "...then they will lose me forever. I choose you, Alistair. I choose you and our kingdom."

Their eyes met and held, then their lips came together in another sizzling kiss. Cinnamon and sweet, the flavor she'd come to associate with her dragon's fond choice of whiskey, greeted the tip of her tongue when she claimed his mouth. "I

VIVIENNE SAVAGE

love you, and nothing will ever keep me from coming back to you."

"Then perhaps I should come in this guise as a human."

"That may be for the best until you've worked your charming magic and taught him the error of his ways. You'll be the lost king of Cairn Ocland."

"We'll arrive with bags of gold."

"The treasure you gifted me to take," Ana said.

Alistair grinned. "It seems it was meant for some greater use after all. If only he had told me, if he had asked, I might have understood and given him what he needed."

"My father is a king, and such men are not in the habit of asking for anything," she replied.

"Perhaps not." His chagrined expression remained.

"And you were not in the habit of giving, my love." She stroked his chest and smiled up at him. "You were a different person then, trapped in a body you had come to despise."

"It is good to stand as a man again," he agreed. "I remain a dragon, but this freedom means everything to me."

"Alis—"

"I am not finished," he said in an impassioned voice. "I once thought I would give anything to have this body returned to me. And then I met you, Anastasia. You. Of all the things I would gladly have abandoned, you are the one thing I could never sacrifice. You've brought me hope and happiness beyond any measurement, lass."

The anxiety she had felt vanished, replaced by a warm,

expanding sensation of hope. Blinking rapidly to clear her eyes of the moisture stinging them, she viewed her new husband through a haze of emotion.

Would her father accept any act of kindness from his former adversary? Could he open his heart to the man who treated her with tenderness, love, and respect as a woman instead of a trophy or possession to be won?

"My father should be honored to have you," she whispered. "I certainly am."

As Anastasia leaned on her tiptoes and kissed him, she knew regardless of the outcome in Creag Morden, Alistair's castle was where she belonged.

Alistair and Anastasia rode some of the way to the kingdom by carriage, landing outside of a smaller village to the south then purchasing fare to the north in a luxury coach.

Since Oclanders were no longer a common sight in any of the western kingdoms, his heathen appearance put them on the odd end of countless stares. Or maybe it was the state of their royal dress, and that he'd donned what he called his finest garments. His kilt was all green tartan and the protective, thick leather worn into battle. And he wore another leather tunic beneath his green plaid sash with polished gold buckles and fastenings.

And when her so-called barbarian husband finished donning it all, she'd struggled against the desire to rip it off of

VIVIENNE SAVAGE

him again. Together, it was finer than the most sophisticated noble garb in Creag Morden, better than silk frocks with gold buttons and velvet surcoats over fancy tunics.

Would her father receive him well? Excluding a pair of brothers running one of the taverns, no one in Lorehaven had seen a man from Ocland in traditional garb in nearly two decades. Shivering, she drew her shawl around her shoulders. The green plaid pattern matched the knee-length garment around his hips, a gift given to all new brides of Ocland. She matched her new husband and wore it proudly.

Three evenings of travel by carriage brought them to the kingdom's capital bright and early. She saw the city through the windows and worried her lip with her teeth. The guards would no doubt recognize her at the city gate as their princess.

But she was now a queen.

"Halt," a guard called in an authoritative, booming voice. "Who travels here?"

"King and Queen TalDrach of Cairn Ocland."

One of the guards laughed. "Did you hear that, Walt? We've got royalty on this coach."

"Where's their royal entourage? Their guards?"

"I thought all of the Oclanders died a few years ago."

Had news from Dalborough not yet traveled to them? She imagined King Frederick and Brunhilda were in mourning, perhaps too inconsolable to share the news of their son's defeat if news had reached them. But with a crippled army and no court magician, she wouldn't be surprised if the survivors were still limping back to civilization.

"Be gone with you," the guard told the driver. "We don't need any eastern beggars sucking what little's left of our coffers dry."

Alistair stiffened. "Beggars?" He moved forward for the door, but Anastasia halted him with one hand on his chest.

"I'll handle this." She threw open the carriage doors and hopped down.

"Does my father know how poorly you treat guests of our kingdom?" she demanded. "Has so much changed in the time since I've left Creag Morden?"

Four sets of eyes grew large and round. "Princess Anastasia?"

"Queen Anastasia to you, and I haven't come to beg anything from my father. I come with wealth—" She tossed a handful of gold coins from their pouch to the ground at their feet. "—and a desire to share my newfound prosperity."

"Your Majesty, I had—we had no idea."

"Forgive us, Your Highness."

"Be thankful it was I, and not my husband, who speaks to you now." She heard Alistair chuckle from within the coach. "I wish to surprise my parents. Now move aside and grant us entry to the city at once."

"Yes, yes of course."

Her king offered his hand and pulled her into the coach when she returned alongside it. Two of the guards opened the immense gates, while the others hastily plucked the discarded

VIVIENNE SAVAGE

coins from the soil.

"You handled that like a true queen," Alistair murmured against her ear. He nipped the sensitive shell, making her shiver.

"They'll show the next guests more respect, that's for certain. Beggars. Hmph."

After another similar encounter at the castle gates, they were admitted onto the grounds and escorted to the doors of the king's receiving room where she hesitated with her fingers on the wood panel.

"You've come so far, lass. There's only one step left," Alistair coaxed her.

A gentle, feminine voice spoke up behind them. "Princess?"

She turned to see a young housecleaner she remembered only faintly.

"Beryl, isn't it?"

"Yes, Your Highness." The maid wrung her hands together. "I must warn you, Princess Anastasia, the months have been unkind to our king. He no longer eats. We force him to accept broth and bread on occasion, but his appetite is spoilt."

"Then leave it to me," Ana said. She strode forward into the audience chamber, determination putting steel into her spine. Alistair moved at her right, the dependable rock she counted on.

"Anastasia?"

Time had changed her father, but not for the better. He

slumped in his throne, face haggard and hair streaked with more gray than she remembered. His ill-fitting clothing had seen better days, loose on a frame lacking his former sturdy bulk.

She swallowed nervously, only to open her mouth and lose her voice. Alistair squeezed her hand, and his encouragement imparted all of the strength she'd needed. "Hello, Father."

"Anastasia!"

He rose and stumbled forward, prompting Ana to rush to his aid.

"I thought I would never see you again."

All of her resentment and hate melted away. She hugged him tight, aware of how thin he felt in her arms. Fragile. No longer the great warrior who had once carried her on his shoulders, but a frail old man worn sick from worry.

"But the dragon...," Morgan whispered. "Ana, I saw the dragon take you away. Did King Frederick keep his word then? Did they truly conquer that bloodthirsty beast and return you to me?"

"No, Papa," she murmured. "Beast is my friend. My dearest friend."

Her father's grip on her tightened and his eyes went wild. "Friend? Ana, no dragon is a friend. What foul magic—"

"Papa, stop and listen to me. I am under no spell. No coercion." She glanced over her shoulder, then back to her father. "And I've brought someone I sorely wish for you to meet."

As Alistair stepped forward, she swept her arm toward him in a flourish and stepped back to place her hand on his upper arm. "King Alistair of Cairn Ocland."

"Cairn Ocland?" Her father's brows rose high on his forehead. "That royal line was wiped out years ago."

"I am quite alive and well," Alistair said. "Much to the disappointment of King Frederick, whose line is in true danger of ending."

"I…." Morgan blinked and looked between them in confusion. "I am not certain I understand. Prince Edward was on the mend and preparing to rescue you. I went to them after you were taken, Ana. I went to them and begged their aid to get you back."

"Prince Edward is dead, Papa. Dead at my hands. He tried to kill me when he led their army to Benthwaite Castle." Her palms grew slick with sweat. "I finished what I began when he tried to rape me the night prior to our wedding."

What little color King Morgan had drained from his face, and beside her, Alistair clenched his jaw. She'd already told him the full story, but his rage renewed. "He said he only claimed a kiss." Her admission aged him further, his features ashen, wrinkles more pronounced.

"He lied to you. He was an awful man, and I defended myself. I didn't think I could ever forgive you for giving me to those horrible people, but you're my father, and you gave me years of devotion and love. And I missed you."

"I never… I thought they would love you no less than we

do, Anastasia. You must believe me. I've wanted nothing more than to save you since the day that beast—"

"Papa—"

"When Sterling disappeared, I thought we had lost the last piece of you we had in this castle. I've lost the faith of the kingdom. Your mother loathes me. All has been lost since the day I betrothed you to Dalborough." His shoulders shook.

"Sterling is safely at home in Cairn Ocland. As for Mother...." She looked to her husband.

Alistair bowed deeply, then removed a single package wrapped in linen from within his sash. "As a token of my appreciation to you, King Morgan, I have brought this gift from my personal garden." He unfolded the square of fabric to reveal a dried twilight rose.

"Is that...?"

"The cure for Mother," Ana whispered. "All we need to do is brew the dried petals into a tea."

"It's... but the beast?"

"I told you, Papa. He's a friend." She laced her fingers in Alistair's hand and smiled up at him. "And we've brought other gifts as well."

Two guardsmen had carried in the trunk from the carriage. Anxious to share her surprise with him, she led her father over to the oversized chest. When she raised the lid, one of the castle guards gasped. Sunlight shone radiant over the surface of hundreds of gold coins. Jewels gleamed in a variety of colors, shapes, and sizes, cut to a polished perfection.

VIVIENNE SAVAGE

"There's enough gold to get your kingdom on its feet again, King Morgan," Alistair said.

Her broken, once powerful father stared at them both with tears in his eyes. "Why? Why would you bring us such wealth?"

"Because he is my husband, Papa."

Alistair raised her hand to his lips and kissed her knuckles before turning his bright eyes to Morgan. "We're family now, and families help one another when in need. I love your daughter with all of my soul, and by proxy, I must also love you for creating such a magnificent, compassionate woman. In my eyes, she is void of any fault or flaw. She is perfection."

Her father stared at both of them, rendered mute by the magnitude of their gift.

"I don't know what to say."

"Then say nothing at all and help me prepare Mother's tea. It's time she joined us."

Her mother's moods frequently shifted between a state of catatonia and hysteria. In the recent months, she'd grown increasingly quiet. The maids washed and dressed her each day, fed her, and moved her through the castle. At other times, she screamed and raged, crying out in pain, hurting herself and even others, burning with an excess of magic that she'd expend with violent spells.

They began drugging her then, deciding her semicomatose state was safer for everyone involved.

"I'm home," Anastasia whispered as she lowered to the edge of Queen Lorelei's bed and took her mother's cool hand.

She sat with her mother throughout the night, dozing in a seat beside the bed after personally administering the sweet and fragrant tea. When his attempts to coax her into bed failed, Alistair joined her in the next chair.

The morning dawned bright and clear, but it paled in comparison to her mother's smiling face. Lorelei awoke a changed woman, as vibrant as Anastasia remembered. They hugged for what seemed like hours and lay together in the bed while Alistair hurried off to find a healer. Ana sobbed against her mother's shoulder while recounting the events of the past two years. It turned out the queen could remember nothing of the time since her dementia reached its peak, save sporadic moments of coherent thoughts concerning her daughter.

Her husband's mistakes and his intention to bind Ana to Dalborough shone like a beacon among Lorelei's foggy recollections. For her, the time had passed like a dream, never knowing what was real and what was a figment of her diminishing mind.

"Mother, I missed you."

"I never meant for you to be tied to that terrible family," Lorelei told her. "I tried... I know I tried to make him stop."

"That's why you both left. Your fit," Ana murmured. Her throat tightened, and she squeezed her mother's hand, kissing the woman's long fingers. "Get some rest. We'll talk more

VIVIENNE SAVAGE

about it later."

"I've spent enough time in bed," Lorelei disagreed. "I want to enjoy tea in the garden with my daughter. Now help me dress. We won't wait for the maids."

"Oh, Mother, I have so many wonderful things to tell you."

Alistair joined Lorelei and Anastasia in the garden for tea where introductions were made. Lorelei instantly fell in love with him, charmed by his good manners and handsome qualities, above all else, she adored him for treating her daughter well. Suddenly, the unyielding and stern mother of her childhood memories was a figment of Ana's imagination.

A courier announced Victoria's imminent arrival, prompting Ana to excuse herself to greet her cousin personally at the front doors.

"When I heard you'd been returned, I couldn't believe it," Victoria cried. She hugged Ana tight. "And married! How did you ever escape that awful dragon and find yourself a husband all at the same time?"

"The dragon wasn't so awful," she confided. "He was rightfully upset that we invaded his home trying to steal. As for the husband...."

They chatted as they strolled through the halls. On their way through the castle to rejoin her parents and Alistair on the veranda, Anastasia glanced into the dining hall. Her father had scheduled an impromptu, celebratory feast to welcome Lorelei home to them and to honor their new alliance with

Cairn Ocland.

A pair of maids paused in the midst of setting the grand table with fine china for a multi-course meal. Her brothers were attending a preparatory school for young nobles halfway across the kingdom, and the table looked too massive for so few chairs and plates.

Anastasia frowned.

"Is there something wrong, Your Majesty?" one asked.

"Yes. This banquet table is completely impersonal. I'll have to shout down the length of the room to talk to anyone."

"Milady, this is how it's always been," the maid fretted.

"I know, but not tonight. I want to be beside my family. To hell with proper seating arrangements," Anastasia declared. She took charge of the maids and joined them in setting the table the way she desired to bring her family closer together. She shuffled the seating arrangements and moved the chairs closer together, shortening the traditional but formal distance between them.

"I can't blame you," Victoria said. "If I had a husband half as handsome as you claim, I'd want to sit beside him, too."

"Come home with us," Anastasia urged her cousin. "And we'll find you an Oclander of your own." Her cousin was well beyond marrying age, a spinster by their standards despite her sizable, generous dowry.

"Do you really mean it?"

"If your parents don't object."

Victoria squealed in delight, throwing her arms around

Ana's neck. "Of course I'll come. They'll let me. They have to!"

Ana laughed at Victoria's enthusiasm but shared her excitement.

"It's good to hear laughter in this castle again." Her father stepped into the room, followed by his wife and Alistair. Victoria's eyes nearly popped from her head.

Ana made introductions and tried not to laugh at her smitten cousin when Alistair took her hand, bowed, and kissed her knuckles.

"You truly weren't lying," Victoria whispered. "Are there more like him?"

"Oh yes. The men of Cairn Ocland are a breed all their own."

A bell chimed outside, announcing the dinner hour. King Morgan clapped his hands together and gestured to the table, only to knit his brows in confusion. "I would invite everyone to be seated but I am not certain what happened here."

"Meals in Cairn Ocland are less formal, Father, and I thought it would be nice for us all to sit close. Come, you and mother sit here."

She directed everyone to their new seats, placing her parents side by side at the head of the table, Victoria in the seat directly across from her, and Alistair to her right. A voice spoke up from the empty chair to Anastasia's left. "Well, this is nice now, isn't it? Very cozy. I like this. Well done, Anastasia."

Everyone turned toward the voice of the additional diner. Seated among them as if she'd been there all along, was the ancient hag from the forest, her face creased with age and hair white as snow.

"Eleanor?" Ana asked, bewildered.

"Hello, dear. I see you made your way from the forest. Not quite so lost now, are you?" The hag winked.

"Mother, be rid of that ridiculous costume."

"Mother?" Ana looked between Lorelei and Eleanor.

"Anastasia, meet your grandmother."

"Ah. You spoil my fun, Lorelei." Eleanor glanced at Anastasia and whispered, "Does she do this to you as well?"

"Often," Ana said.

"*Mother.*"

"Fine, fine." Eleanor clapped her wrinkled hands together and rainbow shimmers surrounded her in a blinding aura of color. When the brilliant corona faded away, a beautiful woman sat where the hag had been. Lustrous golden hair fell down her back in smooth waves, and her old rags became resplendent silks drifting without the wind to blow them.

"And now you decide to show your face," Alistair grumbled. She returned his glare with a sunny smile.

"Moan and groan if you will, my godson, it makes no difference. My pride for each of you is without limit. I am so thrilled, so happy to have watched you grow and mature over these months." Eos left her seat and stepped forward to kiss Ana's cheek. "You are every bit the woman I knew you would become, grandchild."

"Why didn't you tell me who you were when you aided

me in the forest?"

"And spoil everything?" Eleanor laughed. "You had to make the choices on your own, dear, as Alistair did. And you, Morgan, you've learned humility through a tough and difficult lesson."

"You tortured us all, Eos. For what?" Morgan demanded.

The fairy huffed. "I did no such thing. Perhaps you'll evaluate all of your options before you initiate acts of war against others. The consequences of your arrogance tortured you. Did I not warn you many years ago such would happen if you continued to leap to rash, hotheaded behavior?"

Morgan quieted.

Eos glided next to Alistair and touched his face with both hands. "You conquered your temper, dear boy. And most importantly, you've earned the trust of your citizens once more. You will be every bit the ruler your mother and father were during their time in this world. Be good to these two girls, or I shall return."

"I swear on all that I have," Alistair vowed. "I'll be good to… these two?"

Eos cracked a big smile and faded away with the docile breeze, the wind rustling Ana's hair.

And so the next day, King Morgan announced the marriage of their beloved princess to Cairn Ocland's monarch, and their impending parenthood. With the endless treasure brought by his new son-in-law, the kingdom celebrated for days. Commoners sang in the streets, danced, and sent well-wishes to the new couple.

Prosperity returned to Cairn Ocland, and with the death of the black wizard Rangvald, the curse lifted from the land and green flourished once more. The proud native highlanders began trickling in, returning to reclaim their homes and farms.

The rule of Dragon King Alistair and Witch Queen Anastasia ushered in peace for centuries, but all monarchs eventually grow tired. They stepped back and allowed their children and grandchildren to lead, though some say they can still see their red-haired beauty and her beloved beast soaring high above the skies of Mount Benthwaite.

Where they still live happily ever after.

About the Author

Vivienne Savage is a resident of a small town in rural Texas. Over a cup of tea, she concocts sexy ways for shapeshifters and humans to find their match.

To get on Vivienne's mailing list for news and upates, go online and visit http://viviennesavage.com/newsletter

Other Payne & Taylor Books

SHADOWS FOR A PRINCESS
by Dominique Kristine

A T THE AGE of twenty-eight, Princess Ysolde Westbrook is a spinster duchess, the adopted daughter of Hindera's eccentric monarch. Commoners love their benevolent leader, but the kingdom's gentry take offense to the outsider among them. Amid noble plots and demands for her to marry a local aristocrat, an assassination attempt places her life in peril-- if she will not have one of them for a husband, they would sooner see her dead.

Finding allies in strangers with powerful gifts and even darker secrets, Ysolde must learn what it means to lead and find her own inner strengths. Whether or not she survives the tangled web of treason will determine the fate of her duchy, the royal family, and the kingdom she loves.

Blend the intrigue of Game of Thrones with a touch of Outlander's romance for an adventurous fantasy in a whole new realm of magic. Fans of Diana Gabaldon and George R.R. Martin will love the richly descriptive world of Terraina and its many colorful characters.

Turn the page for a sneak peak of *Shadows for a Princess*....

THE RUNAWAY GIRL

A BITTER WIND CUT through Ysolde's traveling cloak, the fur-lined garment as useless as silk. She shivered and warmed her chilled fingers against Tikiina's neck to no avail— her three-year-old filly was also frigid.

With the feeling lost in her hands and fingers, she would soon be forced to stop. Take shelter. Rest for the night and hope the men pursuing her had also become hopelessly lost in the storm. By now, they had to be making camp in one of the many towers littered across the heartlands.

Above her, the sky remained a perpetual state of gray. The wind howled, shrieking around her and whistling through sparse trees jutting like naked toothpicks from the rocky soil. With the exception of the river dividing the country, hard terrain stretched between the coastline and eastern mountain range, separating the kingdom from its neighboring, enemy nation.

Ysolde pursed her lips. She turned her face against the lining of her hood, felt the black bear fur against her cheeks and nose, and closed her eyes. For all her suffering, it would be worth it to see her mother again.

Ten months ago, Tegau had left to rejoin the Marcogh tribes, leaving behind strict instructions: her child was not to accompany her. Ysolde, barely turned eighteen, had been left behind in the castle with her adopted father, stepsiblings, and vindictive stepmother.

By now, he would have realized his daughter was gone, and there were no doubt hundreds of royal guards combing through the countryside for her. They'd ride over the hills and fan out toward the south, north, and west, hoping to find her.

With each hour of travel, her arguments became more convincing, a self-deprecating determination that the man who raised her had done so out of obligation alone.

It was the right thing to do. Her father's legitimate queen had never wanted Tegau or Ysolde in the castle, although they had been there first for many years as consort and adopted child. As far as Ysolde was concerned, Queen Rhonwen was the usurper who swept into their happy lives and unbalanced their world.

Why had the nobles forced the king's hand and made him marry such an awful woman?

Although the weathermages had forecasted clear skies, the threat of a storm loomed above them on the horizon. She cringed, wishing she'd donned more than riding leathers and a cloak.

The wind howled, seeming to scream, "Turn back! Turn back, child!"

And she wanted to heed the wind's warning. After all, didn't her people worship the winds and the sky? Surely the wind knew more and had seen more than her in all of its many millennia of existence, but more than she desired safety, she wanted to see her mother's smile and feel Tegau's warm, inviting embrace.

It was the right thing to do. Without Tegau there, the king would sleep beside his wife, rather than his consort. Without Ysolde in the home, Aldemar would no longer divide his love among three children, rather than the two born from his seed.

Had he even loved her?

No, it was obligation, responsibility to keep her mother happy, and with Tegau gone, Ysolde would force him no longer, even if he'd been the only father she'd ever known.

And she missed him. She missed him so much that burning tears obscured her vision and great sobs made her choke unsteadily atop her mount.

Sensing her rider's distress, Tikiina veered off the trail to the remnants of an old travelers' encampment. She'd been bred by the wilder tribes, a mere foal when she'd been gifted to Ysolde by a Marcogh chieftain when they'd crossed paths while vacationing in a southern province years ago. One of their children should ride one of their horses, the man had said before he and his people continued on their trail.

"Thank you, friend," she whispered.

She dismounted and kissed Tikiina's velvety nose then made use of the camp. It was an eyesore, but it would do, and by the time she'd collected enough wood, her fingers felt waxy, uncooperative, and stiff. They hurt but were required for magic.

Reaching deep, she summoned a spark of mana from the renewable fount of energy within her soul. Magic bloomed at the tips of her fingers and spiraled in a blaze of red. This she directed to the twigs until they caught and became a magnificent glow.

Ysolde added kindling to the fire and waved her hands, weaving together spells and mystical power until the flames roared. She spread blankets over the cold ground and invited Tikiina to lie with her.

"Come, come," she urged the filly. "It's safe. I'll keep you safe."

With promises and gentle coaxes, the copper-furred creature lay beside her. Ysolde snuggled against her side and tossed a blanket over them.

Could she keep them safe?

She thought so. Why else had she endured years of tutoring at the behest of her adopted father to hone her magical talents?

Although her belly protested its empty state, beast and human companion slept.

Hours later, she roused and packed her belongings. She rolled the blankets, kicked earth over the campfire's embers, and walked beside Tikiina until they found a pasture with a pitiful covering of grass. While the horse pulled up mouthfuls of clover, Ysolde nibbled berries she'd packed from the castle pantry.

Was her father worrying by now? Guilt flooded her. He'd have never allowed her to undertake the journey with permission, and traveling with a retinue of soldiers would have slowed her down.

Their second day went the same as the first, and this time as she made camp, she began to doubt herself. She had no idea where to find the Marcogh, memories of the nomadic tribe hazy at best, and their only city was a distant dream at the end of two or three weeks traveling by horseback. Would they even accept a girl among them who couldn't recall the simplest words in their language?

Ysolde guided them toward a pair of large rocks jutting up from the ground at diagonal angles. Loose shale crunched beneath Tikiina's hooves. Cold and numb, she slid down from the mare's back and began the laborious process of clearing out a spot for them both to lie down. With Tikiina settled, Ysolde collected twigs and sticks for a fire. She managed a few feeble sparks then gave up and tried to keep her meager campfire alive.

"We'll be closer to the forests tomorrow," she told her horse, teeth clattering together. "I think. We'll cross the river and find warm pastures."

She dozed off and on, curled into a tight ball against Tikiina's side.

Awakening to the sound of men in her camp, Ysolde's drowsy eyes opened and took in a blurry sight. Men moved freely in her camp and spoke in low tones. Among them, a familiar voice whispered, "By Ashta's breath…she'd have died of cold. Kinsley, fetch wood for the fire. Trevor, see to Tikiina."

It couldn't be.

King Aldemar himself had come to retrieve his child, and Ysolde had never been happier to see him.

"Father?" She pushed up, blankets falling.

"Ysolde, sweetheart, bless Ashta you're all right."

Worry creased his brow, and shadows stood out beneath his gray eyes. He was dressed for a prolonged hunt, in rich furs and thick leathers. After taking a seat on the cold, hard-packed ground, he put his arm around her to lend his additional warmth. A soldier from his retinue covered Tikiina's back with another blanket and tended to the chilly mare.

"I'm sorry. I'm sorry, Father. I was such a f-fool. I thought…"

"No need to apologize," he said in a quiet voice, more concerned with draping his cloak around her shoulders. "Please never do this again, Ysolde. I beg you."

She could only shiver at first, huddling within the enchanted garment. Her teeth chattered. "How did you find me?"

"I saw your campfire from the hilltop. At least, I thought it was yours I saw, but this couldn't have made so much light." Aldemar rubbed his bearded chin, laced with more silver than brown in recent years. They were stark opposites, she and her fair-skinned father.

"Are you taking me back to the castle? Even af-after I ran away?" Another wave of sadness clenched her throat, ushering in a fresh series of sobs. "I didn't think you'd want me anymore without Mother. I th-thought you'd be glad to be rid of me."

"No, my dear. No," Aldemar said firmly. "I'm bringing you back home. I'm sorry you felt unwelcomed. I never meant for that to happen."

Ysolde had no survival skills, but in minutes, the guardsmen had erected tents, fanned out to collect wood, and set a kettle to boil above the fire. Without the wind cutting through, she warmed more quickly.

Safe and warm, the exhaustion of the day took its toll, weighing down her eyelids. She fought against it and turned her face into her father's shoulder.

"Are we going back now?"

"No, my child, you sleep. We'll head back in the morning."

"But what about Mother? I didn't find her."

Aldemar paused. At first, he said nothing then, in a quieter voice, said, "She'll return one day. When she left the castle, your mother promised she'd come back to us. We must trust in her."

As he gazed into the fire, Ysolde saw more than the monarch of Wysteria's wealthiest kingdom. She saw a lonely man, a man who missed his beloved as much as she missed her mother.

She'd been such a fool.

"I love you, Father."

"I feared the worst when we discovered you missing, Ysolde. Please never do this again. If you have grievances with Rhonwen, bring them to me, and I shall deal with her."

"I promise."

He pillowed her head in his lap and stroked her dark hair, humming the song her mother used to sing to the best of his ability. His familiar, off-key rumble reassured her. As she drifted toward sleep, she overheard low murmurs among the men guarding the camp and feeding her fire.

"It truly did appear larger," one knight mused.

"Like a summer bonfire," another agreed.

"Then let us take it as a sign from the goddess that our princess is to return home."

"Princess?" Ysolde questioned, her voice a sleepy slur. She'd never had a title, only called Lady Ysolde by respectful members of her father's court and servants who tended the castle.

"From this day forward, you will always be equal to my and Rhonwen's children in title. You have always been my little princess, and now the rest of the kingdom shall know it too."